KISSING KATE

Kissing Kate

a novel

Bradford Dillman

2005 FITHIAN PRESS, MCKINLEYVILLE, CALIFORNIA

Book design and typography:
Studio E Books, Santa Barbara, CA, www.studio-e-books.com

Published by Fithian Press
A division of Daniel and Daniel, Publishers, Inc.
Post Office Box 2790
McKinleyville, CA 95519
www.danielpublishing.com

LIBRARY OF CONGRESS CATALOGING-IN-PUBLICATION DATA
Dillman, Bradford, (date)
  Kissing Kate : a novel / by Bradford Dillman.
     p. cm.
  ISBN 1-56474-447-7 (pbk. : alk. paper)
   1. Retirement communities—Fiction. 2. Amateur theater—Fiction.
  3. Older people—Fiction. 4. Rich people—Fiction. 5. Socialites—Fiction.
  6. California—Fiction. 7. Actors—Fiction. I. Title.

PS3554.I4187K57 2005
813'.54—dc22

2004022382

My thanks to:

My editor, John M. Daniel, who has done his utmost to protect me from my excesses.

My graphic artist son, Christopher, whose talent has enriched the cover of every book I've written.

My eternal love, Suzy, who eavesdrops on laughter that warms our empty home.

Kiss Me Kate

Music and Lyrics by Cole Porter
Book by Sam and Bella Spewak
A presentation of
The Romero Players

CAST

Fred Graham/Petruchio	Rolf Victor
Lilli Vanessi/Katherine	Selena Cabot
Lois Lane/Bianca	Bunny Auchincloss
Bill Calhoun/Lucentio	Robin Perkins
Harry Trevor/Baptista	Lord Peter Glenn
Hattie (Lilli's assistant)	Marci Dusek
1st Gangster	Baxter Clarke
2nd Gangster	Hugh Tisdale
Genl. Harrison Howell	Arthur Auchincloss
Gremio (2nd Suitor)	Tad Wismer
Hortenzio (3rd Suitor)	Chauncey Slater
Paul (Fred's Dresser)	Perry Nelson
Pops/Doorman	Chuck Mooney
Ralph (Stage Manager)	Mary Tallmadge

PRODUCTION

Director	Reginald Burbage
Producer/Props	Daisy Burbage
Music Director	Elizabeth Clarke
Choreographer	Velvet Jackson
Stage Manager	Kenneth Holly
Assistant S.M.	Buster Rooney
Set Design	Morgan Ball
Sound	Judge Horace Tallmadge
Wardrobe	Lady Louise Glenn
Lighting	Seymour Katz
Makeup	Mary Tallmadge
Box Office	Ashley and Trevor Faye

KISSING KATE

1

I REMEMBER when the phone rang I was trying to kill a cockroach.

I first noticed the sucker while I was sitting on the john; there he was, flicking his antennae from underneath the shower door. But when I rose to get him he was too fast for me, disappearing down the drain.

Having lived awhile in this toilet the landlord calls an apartment, I've learned a thing or two about survival. To win a battle of wits with a cockroach the key is patience. What you do is turn your back on him, pretend he's not there and he'll get cocky. He'll bait you, intermittently exposing himself like a flasher; when you see that, he's yours. Casually pick up the Oxford Dictionary you use as a doorstop, bide your time, maybe whistling to show you've forgotten all about him, then the next time the critter taunts you—wham!

So this one got a reprieve when I decided to answer the ringing before it activated my answering machine. "Hello?"

"Who loves you, pussycat?"

I didn't know whether to be flattered or pissed off. "Long time, no hear, Anastasia."

"You are never far from my thoughts." Agents are so full of crap, but it comes with the territory. I could visualize her, crossing off my name on a list she makes on a yellow legal pad. "I am the bearer of good news."

"I believe it's been over three months since I last heard your sultry voice."

"Business is lousy, Rolf. Or don't you read the trades?"

"That's *your* job. I'm not into pain."

She snorted mild appreciation. She'd be using a pencil to fluff her raven hair as she checked her watch. Time is money, and you don't waste it on a has-been whose commission can't buy a Starbuck's latté.

"You ready for the news?"

Another breed of teasing cockroach? What the hell. "Sure."

"You have a job."

If I were less jaded I might have burst into tears, but I decided instead to punish her with indifference. "Doing what?"

She snorted again. "Doing what you do best, if we don't count fornication. Once again your voice is in demand."

"Where? Singing what?"

Her exasperated sigh conjured the complete picture, a woman of such Mediterranean complexion she could be misaken for black: the ebony eyes, the dark lipstick, the temperament of an Italian diva in the skin of a divorced single mother.

"The best part you've had in ages, pumpkin," she said. "There aren't that many musicals being done in this millennium, you know."

"So you constantly remind me," I said.

"Did or did I not get you *Oklahoma*, *South Pacific*, *Man of La Mancha*—"

"Does your arm ever get tired, patting yourself on the back?"

"Well, this is more than just another musical, sweetheart; it's fun. It's Cole Porter."

My heart bounded. "Cole—Which Cole Porter? He wrote a gazillion shows."

"The best he ever wrote, that's all. You get to have a blast *and* flaunt those pretty pipes. Are you sitting down? It's *Kiss Me Kate*."

She had me. I remember I saw the show seven—no, eight—

times, always jealous as hell of the lead, a flamboyant character, super-macho, always center stage singing those great numbers. It's the one part I always begged to do and never got, my all-time favorite.

Wait. Knowing Anastasia Popkin, theatrical agent provocateur, sure as hell there's a catch. So I said, "Not so fast. What's the money?"

"Five grand a week, plus a hundred per diem."

Nice. "So the name of the company is—what ? Where—?"

I heard tapdancing. "It's a—how shall I say?—*new* company, based about a hundred miles north of here. In a town called Loma Bella."

Loma Bella's a tourist town populated mostly by old folks, most of them rich. "Okay, who else has been cast? Who's playing Kate?"

The pause, obvious stalling, said this was indeed the catch. "Ah, a singer you haven't heard of. Name of Selena Cabot."

"Then give me a few other names."

She blurted the truth in a rush. "There are no other names, Rolf. You're the only Equity member in the company. They're all local amateurs, a group calling itself the Romero Players."

"Jesus."

"Now, hold it—keep your shorts on. Just hear me out. You're going to be able to keep *all* that per diem, lover, because the group's subsidized by a wealthy old widow who's agreed to put you up for the duration, bed and board, in her mansion."

"Where's that?"

"A place called the Elsinore Country Club. She's gaga over the chance to entertain a Broadway star."

I never actually starred on Broadway, as she damn well knew, but part of this was truth. To give me my due, I appeared there. All the years of vocal training paid off every time an audition got me cast—okay, usually in the chorus, but sometimes as second or third lead. The plum roles I played only in road companies and dinner theater.

Come to think of it, a dinner theater tour ending in L.A. became my last stop. It shames me to remember I was actually excited when we hit Tinseltown, figuring with my voice and looks I'd be a natural for the silver screen.

Schmuck. It never dawned on me that Hollywood musicals are deader than Astaire and Mario Lanza.

"Hello, out there," Anastasia called. "You still listening?"

"Just thinking."

"Does five thousand clams a week sound insulting? Four weeks rehearsal, four weeks performance? Do the math, cupcake. That's thirty-six K, after you deduct my commission. Get real. You sure need the work, and my Sylvia's in private school; her tuition's due."

"It's just that—I dunno. Give me a couple of hours? I'll get back to you."

"Rolf Victor, you are a conceited fool."

And she hung up.

Can't blame her for being ticked off; she's been loyal, after all.

But *amateur* theater, for Chrissake? I can't fall any lower than that.

Unless I stop kidding myself. Just look at this place. One room, the kitchenette with a microwave, and a john. The bed's a convertible couch that's always open; I usually forget and bark a shin walking around it. I never close it up unless it's a day when I plan on making it with some popsy, and that becomes cleaning day, when I wash the dishes stacked in the sink and hide dirty laundry in the closet.

And how romantic is it, whispering sweet nothings in a woman's ear when you're competing with planes flying in and out of LAX?

At least when I was married I led the good life, in a railroad apartment on East 41st, coming home after the theater to a hot meal and Faith. But of course Faith proved to be unfaithful, and it ripped my guts out, shredded my confidence so badly I needed to pop tranquilizers just to walk out on a Goddamn stage, damn near destroyed my life!

Hey. Cool it.

Let's see. Five grand a week. And next year my Equity pension kicks in. Put the two together and it's possible I just might save enough to pay rent on better digs. How's that sound, Petruchio, you aging but still alluring rascal?

I looked over to where my doily was taking the air, pinned to its cushion. It's back to work, old timer.

Anastasia must have been sitting by her phone because she picked it up on the first ring. "You've got a deal," I told her.

She sighed. "I'll close it, bubby. You won't be sorry."

I hoped to hell not. I replaced the receiver, rubbing away aggravation, assembling my thoughts.

Now—Now what was it I was doing?

Oh yeah.

Now for that fucking cockroach.

2

"OF COURSE I should give the man a welcoming party," said Isobel von Braun. "But where? The Cafe Hermosa is convenient, just a few blocks from the Romero. What's your view, Kippy?"

Seated next to her at Table One, Robin Perkins set down his oyster fork, weighing this against other possibilities. "Mmm. But he'll be seeing so much of the theater, won't he? Perhaps we should avoid downtown and offer him a lovelier setting. What's wrong with this?"

"Elsinore?" The woman shrugged her broad shoulders. "But Mr. Victor's staying here at Hydrangea, dear. I'd like to offer him something unique."

The slender man pursed his mouth impishly. "We can *make* it unique, Snookums," he said.

The woman was baffled. "But how?"

"We'll make the event a gala, a costume party!" He squeezed close in excitement. "Oh, it's perfect. We're doing 'The Taming of the Shrew,' are we not? How better to greet our guest than as Elizabethans!"

Isobel von Braun raised a large, jeweled hand to pinch his cheek. "You clever little tyke! The things that go on in that naughty mind!" A look to adjoining tables in the club dining room gave her pause. "But how can we convince members to participate? Many might not want—"

"Oh, but they will!" Kip exulted. "The women will be thrilled to pieces to put on period dresses." He huddled close again. "What I'll do first is call Free Your Fantasy and alert them they'll be receiving a large order—"

"But the men," Isobel objected. "I doubt the men—"

"The men will do precisely what their wives tell them, precious. They always do."

The boxy dowager pressed a hand to her bosom and sighed. "Honestly, dear, the things you think of."

Kip captured the other hand and kissed it resoundingly. "You'll see. It'll be Party of the Year!"

I should have been a stage director, he thought; or maybe I *was* in another incarnation. But dear me, so much needs to be done!

In the club directory I count two hundred and ninety-two ambulatory people. First I must hire a tailor to measure them—

if I were to ask them for their true sizes most men wouldn't know and many women would fudge.

Best do it my way.

Call Robin Perkins anything you want, but never call me stupid. I know most Elsinore males disapprove of me, but screw them.

They cooperate or else, because I'm under the aegis of Isobel von Braun, the club's founding member, thank you very much, and don't you ever forget it, mister. Whatever Isobel wants, Isobel gets—except when she's sabotaged by bitch Selena Cabot.

Well, it took the tailor three days to measure so many people, calling out numbers I jotted down on two hundred and ninety-two prepared cards.

When at last the wardrobe arrived, in cardboard packing boxes, I went to Otto and obtained management's permission to store them in the living room of Cottage Two. He agreed the adjoining bedrooms would be suitable for changing when members tried on the garments.

It took a day to safety-pin two hundred and ninety-two tags, matching the person to the costume. Then I directed club secretary Tiffany to print out a schedule I Scotch-taped to the cottage door, listing the time each person was expected for fitting, so there'd be no congestion.

As expected, the women were all cooperative. As expected, not so their husbands.

"What the hell is this?" a lout named George Kleinsasser demanded, lifting up his hanger.

I replied politely, "It's doublet and hose, sir. All Elizabethan men wore them."

From his expression one would have supposed he was holding road kill. "The doublet—maybe. But I am not going to wrestle myself into this pantyhose unless I wear a jock strap, and I haven't done that since I played ball at Stanford."

Mrs. Kleinsasser intervened. "George, you will do exactly what Mr. Perkins tells you."

And that settled that.

Naturally I reserved the two most regal costumes for Isobel and the Cabot bitch.

Once they emerged from the changing room it was touching, really, to see my fiancée's eager expression, the appeal for approval, so I cried, "Snookums, my heart races. I may perish!"

Of course, she giggled like a schoolgirl.

I made no comment to Cabot. It's unnecessary to tell her she's attractive.

All two hundred and ninety-two actors were asked to carry the costumes to home closets and to dress in them next day for my noon class in Elizabethan behavior. As requested, the throng assembled on the putting green, normally a no-no, permissible today because the cast wore slippers.

When I began speaking, the ladies and scullery maids crowded close to hear, but the lords and vassals paid no attention. The boors may have thought they were putting one over on me, but I noticed their rudeness as, one at a time, they drifted off toward the men's locker room bar.

Addressing their wives, I began, "Our first challenge is the proper way to curtsy." I pantomimed as if wearing a floor-length dress. "We bend our knees to lift the hem of our gown—just so—so we won't soil it by trailing it on the ground."

Then I walked among the overweight, awkward dears, exercising tact, correcting yet always encouraging.

"That's the way... Don't be reluctant to flirt... Squeeze him with your eyes... That's it... Yes... Beautiful, beautiful... Mr. Victor will be overcome. I worry he may sweep you all up in his arms and carry you off!"

I rewarded their titters by blowing kisses.

"You're all to die for. Tonight get plenty of beauty sleep, ravishing creatures, because tomorrow—it's show time!"

3

IT'S A SHORT TRIP by air from L.A. to Loma Bella, just twenty-four minutes, but the first class ticket entitled me to one privilege.

After I was belted in I told the stewardess, "Once we're aloft, kindly bring me a double Dewar's on the rocks."

She frowned disapproval. "We really don't have time, Mr. Victor."

She was a granny, about thirty pounds overweight. Jesus, I can remember when stewardesses were young, pretty and eager to please—the *Coffee, Tea or Me?* years. Now they call themselves flight attendants and act like they're doing you a favor, the women testy, the fruits snippy.

I watched as granny cracked open two mini bottles of Dewar's and poured the scotch over ice in a plastic glass. The first jolt warmed my cockles; relaxed, I reviewed what I'd packed for a two-month stay: the good suit, of course, at least twenty years old but gray flannel never goes out of style; the blue denim trou to go with different golf shirts; and what I'm wearing for the flight, the fawn jogging suit that's never seen sweat—from running, that is—only sweat from rehearsal nerves.

Once the wheels touched down I was feeling rosy, even excited. I didn't know what to expect, but it was my first job in many moons and whoever these people were would know how to spell my name right on the check.

So I shouldered my canvas bag, smiled thanks at the granny, and proceeded down steps to the tarmac. It was a tiny airport; I saw maybe a dozen people standing on grass behind the arrival gate. I was looking for a sign with my name on it when lo and behold who should step forward but Anastasia Popkin. "Surprise," she called.

I was both complimented and pleased. "What in hell are you doing here?"

"Earning my commission," she shouted above whining aircraft. "I drove up to be sure they're giving you the VIP treatment." Her black eyes were glistening, black hair clipped in back, moist black lips inaudible as she tugged me inside the terminal and held out a hand. "Give me your luggage receipts."

"There's just the one." After I ripped it from the ticket envelope she gave it to a starstricken, acne-afflicted girl.

"This is Gretchen, a Romero apprentice," she said. "She'll see it's automatically delivered to your digs at Elsinore."

"Thank you," I called over my shoulder. Popkin now had me by an elbow, hurrying me outside to a gray Rolls Royce parked at the curb. Holding open the rear door was a slim, youngish guy in a khaki summer suit and pink tie.

"Rolf Victor, this is Kip Perkins, the fiancé of your hostess, Isobel von Braun."

"Pleasure," I said, clasping a limp hand. "I'll get in front."

"Nope, the back," said Anastasia. "You're not done with me just yet. I'm riding shotgun all the way to Dodge."

The chauffeur relieved me of the shoulder bag and fastidiously placed it on the front seat. Observing his delicate passage around the hood I wondered if I'd heard right. "So, Kip—" I said as he eased the car into traffic. "You getting married soon?"

"Just as soon as Snookums gives the green light."

Anastasia gripped my knee, a warning. "You should know, Rolf, Mrs. von Braun is the person bankrolling this production. To put it another way, in addition to taking care of your domestic needs, she's paying your salary."

I grimaced. "That's a deep debt. Anything I can do to compensate?"

Popkin laughed. "Behave yourself."

As proof I sat back and half-listened to the dark lady's recital of scenic particulars. "Loma Bella has a building code that dictates all construction must be Spanish style, including tiled roofs. Of course, on the outskirts, where we're headed, you can do whatever your money will buy, and as you'll see there's no shortage of money."

These were gated homes, each with a security warning. Proceeding down an avenue bordered by eucalyptus, on the right I saw a chain link fence topped with barbed wire that gave glimpses of opulence flanking the fairways of a golf course.

"Elsinore," Anastasia announced.

Kip turned off and stopped the Rolls at a security booth. A uniformed man emerged and saluted, saying, "Everything's set, Mr. Perkins." And he signaled to an individual dressed in armor who was holding some sort of brass musical instrument.

"What—?" I began.

"I'll be damned," Popkin said. "I do believe it's a Danish elkhorn."

An electric gate retracted, and as the car inched forward the musician raised the horn to his lips and blew a mournful sound answered a moment later from somewhere below.

A street sign told me we were descending Hamlet Road, probably the main artery. The intersections were named after other characters; I noticed Ophelia Way, Horatio Hollow and Polonius Place before we reached a low building with a spacious parking lot, obviously the clubhouse. Standing at its entrance, also dressed in armor, was the second elkhorn, raised to sound a series of triumphal notes. This caused the double doors to open, releasing an inundation of men and women, all of a certain age, all accoutered as Elizabethans, men in doublet and hose, women in long skirts and kerchiefed hair, carrying baskets of rose petals. The crowd shouted a bedlam of Shakespearean greetings.

"Hey nonny nonny!"

"Ods bodkins!"

"Fie on't!"

They rushed to surround the Rolls and pelt it with petals, as a beaming Kip Perkins, proud parent of children performing in a play, dismounted to open a passenger door.

"My, what fun," Anastasia said uneasily.

"Christ," I said.

The elkhorn sounded again and the crowd stepped back, permitting passage of two stately ladies Popkin introduced to my ear. "The plain one's your hostess, Isobel von Braun. The looker's your leading lady, Selena Cabot." Both wore regal Elizabethan gowns and had flowers in their hair. Prodding my thigh, she purred, "Get out and greet them."

So I complied, careful not to bang my head. Casing the situation I wore my all-purpose fixed smile.

Von Braun advanced and dipped in a deep curtsy. "Let all the number of the stars give light to thy fair way!" she quoted, badly.

The looker swooped next to her. "The stars above us govern our conditions!" she quoted, resonantly.

This cued a trio of strolling musicians—a piercing fife, a lyre, and a tabor drum—to cavort and twist in circles ahead of the two regals who, without invitation, had each claimed one of my arms. At the junction of Hamlet Road and a green (the eighteenth?), two little girls, probably a member's granddaughters, took the lead, skipping ahead, raining more rose petals on the fairway.

I sneaked a peek to the rear. Behind me was a wary Popkin, followed in turn by a clumsy procession of lords and vassals, as their ladies and scullery maids gaily exhausted their baskets. And at the very rear, conspicuous for wearing maintenance uniforms, came the Mexican greenskeepers, spearing the mess off the grass and disposing of it in Hefty bags.

Set up at the intersection were linen-covered tables; all the drinks, alcoholic and non, served in tankards by Latino bartenders embarrassed to be seen wearing tights. The ladies and scullery maids congregated, chirping like birds in congratulation for the originality of their costumes, while the lords and vassals lunged for the bar, elbowing one another aside to place their orders.

As guest of honor I had a queen at each ear. Isobel von Braun was saying, "This Elizabethan motif is a lark, but I must assure you, Mr. Victor, your suite in Hydrangea has all the modern conveniences."

And Cabot was saying, "You see my house just across the fairway—the one with the garret? Anytime you want to run the jokes, my door is open."

Turning from one to the other, I said, "Thank you… You're very kind; thank you." In serious need, I decided to speak up. "Do you suppose—I mean, is it okay if I got myself a drink?"

"No!" Isobel exclaimed. "You will do no such thing. I shall see it is brought you at once. What would you like?"

"If you please, a double Dewar's on the rocks?"

"Done!" And she raised an imperious hand.

As afternoon surrendered to twilight my celebrity citadel was under siege, bombarded by deafening questions from strangers I shrugged away, fighting to maintain a channel to the bar for another double Dewar's. Inevitably backed against a hedge, I was overwhelmed by the breath of a besotted Elizabethan who identified himself as "Trevor Faye!" He pointed at a woman with the smile of a human headlamp. "My wife, Ashley," he shouted.

"Beautiful, beautiful," I shouted back.

"Guess how old she is?"

"Couldn't. Young, though."

A blast of bourbon caused me to wince. "She's sixty-two years old."

"Impossible," I said, looking for escape.

"Yes, she is. And furthermore, you know what?"

"What?"

"We do it every Saturday night!"

I stammered, "Well. Well, lucky you. I believe tomorrow's Saturday." I patted the nincompoop's arm and again shouldered to the bar, holding out my empty glass. "Help, *señor*. Double Dewar's, rocks."

A female voice yelled, "Having fun?"

It was the black ferret, Popkin.

"For God's sake, lady, get me out of here. This is bedlam. There's a fireplug who wants me to lift weights with him, a phony lord who wants me to play golf, a ham who claims he's my director—the aggravation is unending. I want *out*."

Anastasia shook her head, shouting, "I have two words for you, heartthrob. Thirty-six K."

It was after sundown when I realized Kip had me by a sleeve, pulling me toward the entrance of a nearby home. "Hydrangea!" he cried. "Come in, come in." He was dancing ahead past a wall of hydrangeas, past twin beds of carnations that flanked a spackled walkway. "Snookums is ecstatic to be entertaining a Broadway star!"

Thanks a bunch, Anastasia, I thought.

We went down marble steps to a sunken living room where Isobel von Braun, still dressed in royal raiment, still wearing flowers in her hair, was recovering on a couch. "I am exhausted," she announced, "and you must be, too."

"I'd be lying if I claimed otherwise." The moment had arrived to pay for my room and board. "There are no words to tell you, ma'am, how grateful I am for your generosity. To provide a stranger with such hospitality is kindness in the extreme." When necessary nobody can touch me; I lay on charm with a trowel.

Her mouth twitched, an acknowledgment of the tribute. Fatigue heightened her plainness. This was a woman who could not have been pretty even when young.

"Your room is just down the hall, next to mine!" the fiancé trilled.

"You can show him in a moment, Kippy," my hostess said. "First, I'd like a word with Mr. Victor."

"Rolf, ma'am. Please call me Rolf."

She inclined her head. "Kind of you, sir. But I believe in certain formalities."

So much for charm. "Of course. Whatever you prefer."

She rose and took center stage on the thick white carpet. "To give you some history: Hydrangea was the first home built in Elsinore, when my husband Frederic and I settled here twenty-two years ago. It was he who conceived the idea of making *Hamlet* the club's theme. Considering his wealth, people assumed he'd majored in economics at the University of Pennsylvania, when in fact he majored in Shakespeare."

"Interesting. It's sure a beautiful home."

She gestured. "I asked the architect to give it a desert motif—scads of pale browns, as you can see in the furniture and furnishings. Restful colors, don't you agree?"

"More than that, ma'am. I'd say 'soothing.'" Kippy moaned agreement. I had a fan.

"And I specifically requested floor-length glass windows to invite sunlight. A stand of trees affords shade for the patio and also acts as shield from any golf balls that might threaten my windows. As you see, they also open a vista to the lush greens of the golf course and the sparkling blue of my lake. Naturally I realize it's merely a water hazard, but I like to think of it as my lake."

Her pause awaited comment, so I said, "That splashing fountain makes a lovely sound."

"Yes, restful, don't you agree?"

"Absolutely. Also soothing." Her stare made me suspect she smelled crap, so I quickly asked, "Is this the eighteenth hole?"

"Yes, the finishing hole. Golfers must decide whether to lay up short of the lake or risk carrying it to reach the green. Every month dozens of balls are retrieved from my lake. Do you play, Mr. Victor?"

"Seldom, ma'am. Don't have much time. And when I do play, I play badly."

She rewarded me with her first genuine smile. "You have just described my own game." Just as swiftly the smile disappeared. "Now then—it's too dark to see at present, but tomorrow you will notice a French provincial monstrosity facing us directly across the fairway, a house with a garret above. You should know that is the residence of Selena Cabot, the woman cast as your leading lady."

She paused. Invitation for me to comment? "Yes, we met during the festivities; briefly, I regret to say. But I'm sure I'll—"

"Selena is one of my most treasured friends, but I must verbalize a teensy warning, because she most certainly will find you attractive, and that could be dangerous."

"Dangerous?"

She scowled alarmingly. "Beware. All three of Selena's husbands died under highly mysterious circumstances."

I was puzzling that remark when she moved to another window. "And tomorrow you will also see my swimming pool. I tell guests who enjoy sunbathing they can find all the seclusion they wish, hidden from inquisitive eyes by three walls of hedge. Should you seek sun or isolation, the sanctuary is yours, day and night."

"I've never been so spoiled."

She was yielding to exhaustion. "Kippy will show you to your room. I am confident you will find the accommodations comfortable, but if there's anything I have omitted to make your stay more pleasurable, kindly say so at once."

The ersatz fiancé piped up. "Snookums?"

"Yes, Kippy?"

"Remember it's Wong's night off. Should I call the club to reserve a table?"

Fatigue placed second to graciousness. Inhaling energy, she answered, "Yes, dear. And ask Otto for Table One before a certain person gets the same idea."

4

IN RETROSPECT isn't it ironic, Selena mused, that originally Isobel and I were the closest of friends? Perhaps the bonding occurred because we were of similar age (she *claims* to be only three years older than I, which would make her fifty-five, but at Wellesley she may have majored in fiction). Perhaps it occurred because we both had married older men. Perhaps it occurred because of the misfortunes that befell our husbands. Precious Carter had his seizure two years before Isobel's husband suffered a stroke during a club ball benefiting the Museum of Natural History. Though nearing eighty years of age, Frederick von Braun, a numbingly boring man forever spouting Elizabethan gibberish, was performing a duty dance with the last of the ladies at his table when the orchestra segued from a slow fox trot to a schottische. He was hopping gamely until his collapse.

Typically, von Braun chooses not to remember, but it was I who assumed domestic supervision of the stricken couple, I who

hired the male nurse, the slender but surprisingly strong Robin
Perkins. Too ill to protest being hefted out of wheelchairs onto
toilets and into beds, Frederick remained irascible to the end,
dark glowers manifesting his disapproval of the nurse. So perhaps it was best he never saw Robin mourning over his coffin at
Loma Bella Cemetery, in a plot just five doors down from Carter's, in the premier row on a bluff overlooking the channel, the
majestic San Gregorio mountains behind. Yes, perhaps it was
best he never saw the little man become an enduring household
legacy. He'd have suspected Kip's motives, zealous in protection
of the fortune amassed at Pittsburgh Screw and Bolt, an amount
to match the many millions bequeathed me by dear Carter.

To assuage Isobel's bereavement I prescribed the activity of
bridge tournaments and charity luncheons. We became insepa-
rable, sharing two bonds—childlessness and an appetite for gossip. The pair of us rejoiced to see our whispers redden ears all
over Elsinore.

Isobel became vulnerable the day she justified Kip's abiding
presence in Hydrangea as pre-nuptial. I abstained from comment on condition she refrain from airing scandalous particulars
of my brother, Hugh Tisdale. Though the bargain was sealed
with a handshake, it doesn't prevent von Braun from periodical-
ly poking me off-balance; only a lioness has a keener scent for
disabled prey. "I despair, darling, that we see so little of your
brother. Why isn't he living with you? You have scads of room."

I moved crosswind, sighing, "Believe me, I've begged him.
But the boy so values his independence."

As proof, I rented Hugh a tiny apartment near Safeway su-
permarket, a sufficient distance to avoid contaminating my own
reputation, because I'd learned he was so tormented by hyperactive hormones his sole interest in life was sex.

The particulars of what was to be first in a sequence of humiliating episodes were reluctantly conveyed by Dr. Milo Fish, an

Elsinorean serving on the Mercy Hospital Board. It was the discovery of Hugh in a fourth floor linen closet with a notorious nurse, the pair locked in strenuous copulation atop a mound of soiled sheets.

This, and subequent amatory adventures were never, of course, described in the Loma Bella *Sun*. Nevertheless Elsinore was alive with whispers that mortified me and infected Hugh's chances for club membership.

These thoughts were uppermost in my mind the morning I found myself hoisted on my own petard. Taking a shortcut, thinking the club card room would be unoccupied at so early an hour, I came face to face with my accomplice.

I can't help it. Isobel's round neck and hunched shoulders have always reminded me of a cobra coiled to strike. Sibilance enhances the impression, an unsettling hiss. "This Mr. Victor," the woman hissed, "your leading man, must be dazzled by your show business background, dear."

This was clearly an invitation to gossip, one I tactfully declined. Dodging like a mongoose, I escaped by saying, "Thank heaven dear Carter saved me from a lifetime of disappointment. Pity you knew him but briefly, love, because he was known as the Wizard of Wall Street. His stunning investments made further employment unnecessary." Absently fingering my diamond engagement headlight, I hurried on my way.

Such a common woman could never appreciate a class act like Carter. His adoration began the night he saw me at the Winter Garden, when he dispatched his chauffeur to buy two dozen red roses and a bottle of Dom Perignon so he might have them at the ready, offering them so humbly, so sweetly, when I emerged out the stage door.

Once he proposed marriage, once I was certain my name would change from Tisdale to Cabot, it terminated the quarrel I'd been having with Mumsy and Da-da about pursuing a stage career. Of course, in exchange for financial security I bought trouble. The marriage's drawbacks numbered six, the beastly brats from his earlier union. Who do you suppose inherited the responsibility of remembering their birthdays and choosing their gifts at Christmas? Predictably, the brats, now grown to adult misbehavior, were infuriated when the lawyer read the will leaving me ninety percent of Carter's fortune. But that's how he wanted it, because he loved me until the day he died.

Or night, rather.

Naturally, being of advanced age and somewhat frail, Carter was never overly demanding in the bedroom, but he remained infatuated with what he called my "long-stemmed roses," my shapely legs, right to the end. In fact, it was following an especially gay dinner at Table One, entertaining Baron and Baroness Manstein, that he expressed a desire to top off the evening, as it were, with an act of homage. The old dear was doing his best, bless him, until finally expending his tribute in a curious sigh— of satisfaction, I supposed, but no. The sigh deepened to a rattle and suddenly Carter collapsed.

The papers reported my husband had died peacefully in his sleep. Of course, chatterbox von Braun would give her Wellesley diploma to know the authentic particulars of his passing, but not bloody likely, mate. The secret's interred forever in Loma Bella cemetery.

OKAY.

I get myself in a situation where I'm dealing with hard-core amateurs, where I've accepted room and board from one snob, been cast opposite another, and the two apparently despise each other. So where do we go from here?

To yet *another* welcoming party, that's where. And sure enough, catered by club manager Otto Steiner, who did all the hand-kissing last night at Table One. He's something else, this guy; when he's not bowing and scraping he stands like a poker's up his ass. My guess is, his German accent is an act; he fakes it because he knows rich women like their maître d's to sound foreign. What do you bet old Otto was born in Cucamonga and majored in drama at Long Beach State?

One thing for sure, he knows the most important hand to kiss, nibbling the jewelry of Isobel von Braun, who's sponsored this "Getting To Know You" bash in the club ballroom. It's crushing chaos, a mixture of guests and harried waiters and waitresses, taking drink orders and passing trays of hors d'oeuvres. Judging by their laughs and shouts, the suits and dresses are insiders, surely uninterested in saying hello to a stranger who smells of show biz.

"I can't hear a damned thing, Kip," I yell. "Do me a favor? Let me know when I shake a hand that's important?"

He squeezes my arm and leads me out of the snake pit into an empty buffet parlor. The closed door muffles the din. He says, "Sir, it's only fitting I bring the important people to *you*." Can you beat it? Kippy's decided he loves me.

So I'm standing there like Father Damien on Molokai, when the door opens again, giving entrance to a familiar face dimly remembered among the Elizabethans, now decked out in a safari suit, an ascot tied at the neck. The middle-aged peacock advances in a strut, submitting a smirk probably intended as a smile.

At arm's length he thrusts out a hand. "Once again welcome, dear boy. You may be kind enough to recall that I am Reggie Burbage, director of the Romero Theater. Jolly glad you survived last night." His articulation is flawless British thespian, savoring words as so many morsels of caviar.

"Looking forward to working with you," I lie.

"Incredibly generous of your hostess to be *Kate's* patron saint, though usually Isobel is indifferent to Romero offerings. Frankly I'm hoping this experience might encourage her to subsidize our year-round schedule, some six productions a year, one succeeding another—rather like the Old Vic, or what you Americans call 'summer stock'."

I polish off the scotch. "Stock. Yeah, I did that. Did you act with the Old Vic?"

He chuckles in self-deprecation. "No, no, gracious no, though some have flattered me by suggesting I might have. I did meet Larry Olivier once and shared a most stimulating conversation about the rigors of repertory theater. Larry directed as well as acted, too, you know, so in that regard we had much in common."

A thought crosses my mind that should be voiced. "I take it you've had a lot of experience directing musical comedy?"

He fidgets, frowning. "Ah, to share a confidence, Rolf, this is a fresh challenge for me. I'm a bit nervous about it, actually, this being the first musical the Romero's ever staged."

Another thought needs to be voiced. "Will you also be performing?"

He smiles regret. "I fear my singing is unequal to the task, and I'm too old to leap about as a dancer. No, unhappily I must sit this one out and instead bask in the laurels I received in our most recent production."

"What play was that?"

He inhales pride. "*A Streetcar Named Desire*. One can't do better than that, can one, staging a Tennessee Williams classic? What an absolute peach of a part!"

I have a sense of foreboding. To release the question I clear my throat. "What part was that?"

Burbage appears astonished. "Who else, old boy? I was Stanley Kowalski."

On cue, Kip appears, bearing a double Dewar's, bless his heart.

"My savior," I tell him, accepting the manna, again turning my attention to Burbage. "You don't suppose there's a likelihood my leading lady's in attendance?"

He frowns. "Fashionably late as usual, I fear. But not to worry, old bean, she's a consummate professional. Has never missed an entrance."

A blast of noise tells me someone's come to pay respects, in this case two people, a round little woman escorted by a blocky guy who looks like his suit's on too tight.

"Ah!" Burbage exlaims. "My superb musical director." He sweeps an arm in presentation. "Libby Clarke and her husband Baxter."

As expected, he has a crushing grip. He says, "We met last night. I'm playing First Gangster."

"Great part, fun part," I say, kneading my knuckles. "You work out a lot, sir?"

He misses the sarcasm, saying seriously, "Every single day. Check out my gym at Bowflex."

"Where?"

"Bowflex."

I don't get it.

"It's my home," he says.

I focus on the tiny woman—music director, did he say? She's shaped like a volley ball, round-shouldered from supporting such enormous boobs. I say, "Am I safe in assuming Bowflex includes a piano?"

She giggles as if I'd told a joke, then sobers up. "This must be terribly difficult for you, Mr. Victor, a singer accustomed, I'm sure, to the accompaniment of a full orchestra."

"Well, yeah. But what—I don't understand—"

"I shall do my utmost to give your voice the assistance it deserves."

"Well, thank you." I'm standing perplexed when she makes way for another couple, introduced by another blast of noise, a

woman transparently accustomed to making an entrance, together with a geezer at least forty years her senior. He's smiling
like a simpleton, probably hoping conspicuous hearing aids will
discourage conversation.

"Aaah!" Burbage cries. He's a master at conveying pleased
surpise. "Lucky Rolf, meet the queen of the Romero Theater,
my long-time leading lady and muse, Mary Tallmadge. I'm
thrilled to inform you I've cast her as Bianca."

She's russet-haired and poised. As I shake her hand she says,
"I've listened to the CD of your work; frankly I'm intimidated to
be sharing the same stage with you." Like Reggie's, her accent is
British. "This is my husband, Judge Horace." The relic nods,
not having heard.

My director turns emcee. "Mary and I have performed together countless times. I'm immodest enough to tell you, old
goose, she and I have been compared favorably to Lunt and
Fontanne." She lowers her eyes modestly. "When I told her
she'd be playing Bianca, she demurred, protesting she's never
done a musical. Well, of course I'd have none of that. I said,
'You mean the most haunting speaking voice ever to fill a theater can't manage a speck of vibrato?'"

"I hope you'll be patient with me, Mr. Victor." Burbage is
right. The voice is husky and so resonant its whisper would be
heard in the back row. The Lunt and Fontanne analogy could
be stretching it, but it's plain to see she'd definitely match the
ham's invincible poise.

"Please call me Rolf. And if I may—Mary?" She nods. "Are
you from England originally?"

"Yes. Bournemouth, if you know where that is. It's only fair
you should hear my resumé. I trained at the Royal Academy and
spent many years in rep and on the West End before foolishly
accepting a contract at Metro-Goldwyn-Mayer."

"I thought I recognized—"

"No. No, you wouldn't recognize me. I played British nannies, pushing prams for Kathryn Grayson. The best decision I ever made was to move to Loma Bella and become a big fish in a small pond." She frowns. "I worry about my present assignment. I believe Reggie's expecting too much."

"It's only a musical," I joke.

She's in no mood for humor. "Forgive us, Rolf, but Horace and I must leave. We're accustomed to dining early. Just wanted to pay our respects."

"It's been my pleasure," I say, watching her exit, thinking, why did such a pretty lady opt for an ancient? He must be worth megabucks.

I notice I'm low on Dewar's when I hear another gust of noise and see another familiar face. It's one Queen for a Day, Selena Cabot, now wearing a green satin dress that probably cost more than a year's rent in El Segundo. She fixes me in her sights and fires immediately, saying, "You're younger than I expected."

How about that? No intro. No "I believe we met earlier" or "Welcome to Loma Bella." Just wham, brassy and sassy. So I fire back, "Weren't you ever told it's impolite for actors to talk about age?" As if I'd point out she's concealed miles with cosmetic surgery. But make no mistake, she's a raven-haired stunner; about fifty, as a guess. She carries herself with an easy arrogance that says, if she so chose, she'd wear you out in bed.

"I love it!" Kip cries. "The hostility! The very incarnation of Lunt and Fontanne, the models for your characters. Offstage they loathed each other."

"Wait a minute. I have no hos—" I begin, stupidly defending myself. "On the contrary, it's my privilege to share the stage with Ms. Cabot."

"I played your CD," she says. "You have a helluva baritone."

"Thank you."

"But I have no CD to play for you. Instead, I have to fall back on a summary of my credits." She ticks off a rehearsed bio. "I began as a Rockette at Radio City Music Hall, then branched out into chorus work on and off Broadway—"

"As a matter of fact, that's exactly how I—"

"You'll find I have a big voice—not Ethel Merman, mind—but over the years I held my own singing with the best."

"Oh, I'm sure you're—"

She holds up a hand. "Hold it a second, here's the catch. The catch is, I haven't done it in years. When I was in my twenties I married a wealthy man who made employment of any kind unnecessary, and now, all these years later, my hunger for the theater has come back. I'd return every piece of jewelry lavished on me, if only I might reclaim the opportunities I squandered as a girl."

Selena is astonished by her own behavior. Why are you carrying on like this? The man hasn't asked you to justify anything, hasn't asked you to explain this impetuous decision. He signed on to make some easy money, that's all, knowing he was involving himself with amateurs, probably expecting the worst. Well, I have a surprise for him.

We'll sure make a handsome couple onstage. I'd guess he's somewhere in his late fifties, and you can see he's a presence, tall, broad-shouldered, and still endowed with a full head of salt-and-pepper hair. Oh yes, Elsinore's menopause set is in for a treat.

Providing Burbage proves he knows more about directing than he does acting. Well, it's mainly a traffic assignment, after all, keeping members of the chorus from colliding with one another. But I worry about the casting. He's even given my brother Hugh a part, for God's sake.

I speak up. "Reggie, are you certain Hugh Tisdale is qualified to be involved in this?"

"The role is Second Gangster, dear girl. No vocalizing required beyond 'Brush Up Your Shakespeare,' and those lyrics, he can shout."

Well, it might keep him out of trouble, my little brother, my crown of thorns, whose hyperactive hormones are an ongoing embarrassment. Gossips will never let me live down his fling with the married checker at Safeway, recounting the scene when her husband surprised him, causing him to jump out the bedroom window into a patch of poison oak.

Oh, some people found it amusing, like the emergency staff at Mercy hospital, and of course Isobel von Braun, forced to hold her tattling tongue under terms of our agreement. But Mumsy and Da-da would have been mortified.

Just a moment. What right do they have to be judgmental? What right, precious parents, do you have to cast stones, having created Hugh eleven long years after me? What were you thinking? Or did it happen because you'd been drinking?

You must have guessed his worthlessness, bequeathing him the trust fund. But why oh why did you have to name me as executrix, to oversee an annual allowance Hugh exceeds without fail?

Enough of this self-pity. Perhaps it's for the best Burbage has included baby brother. I can keep an eye out, quash any moves he makes on chorines from U.C. Loma Bella, and tattletale Isobel must keep out of it.

In return I'll uphold my end of the deal and say nothing critical about Robin Perkins, the blatant homosexual she passes off as her fiancé. Well, I ask you, what man would escort such a tedious woman to parties otherwise? He's harmless enough.

"Penny for your thoughts, enchanting Selena."

I awaken. "Forgive the daydreaming, Reg. Remind me again, please, the exact role Isobel insisted be reserved for her fiancé?"

He squirms at the question, as intended. The witch's financial support of this musical emasculates his credibility totally.

"Kip is doing Lucentio, opposite Mary Tallmadge's Bianca."

While he's wriggling I get in one more dig. "But can he sing? Does he dance?"

He harrumphs. "Well—well, he's not professional, of course, but then the same can be said for almost everyone else with the exception of you and Rolf. I *have* observed him, as perhaps you have, braying away whilst whirling ladies 'round the club dance floor."

"Yes. Yes, I've witnessed that performance many times."

Rolf Victor laughs, reminding me he's been eavesdropping on the doubletalk and finds it amusing. He really is an attractive man, I decide, and perhaps he'll want to rehearse during off hours, so I tell him, "My house is directly across the fairway from where you're staying. You're welcome to come over for a drink, run lines or whatever, whenever."

He nods thanks. "Very thoughtful, Selena."

"Next to Isobel's, Versailles is the oldest home in the club. My husband Carter and I were the second couple to build here; it was he who insisted I devote full time to our marriage. When he died—"

What's this? A flashback to circumstances of the event that I must blink away.

"—after he left me, once I was alone, I had an awful time getting the Board's permission to add a garret, a sanctuary where I paint, meditate, enjoy cooling winds from the channel, or just admire the San Gregorio mountains. It's a stunning view."

A view that surmounts von Braun's hydrangeas, where I can see the comings and goings of her tacky guests.

Burbage interrupts. "I think we've monopolized Rolf long enough. Terribly selfish of us, you agree? Let's allow him liberty to mingle with Isobel's guests."

I signify agreement by taking Rolf's hand. No wedding ring.

I squeeze it, saying, "Stay at my side and no one will dare harm you."

He's smiling when the door opens, admitting a frightful din.

Seymour Katz was never one to contribute to din. Unobtrusive as always, he was just another seersucker jacket in the crowd. The man avoided mingling because he was by nature shy, his fastened pleasant expression behind spectacles discouraged approach, and those people at the party he did know were loath to converse with him.

For Seymour Katz was a cosmetic surgeon.

Clients so trusted his discretion they could only surmise which guests had benefited from his knife. Looking around, sipping Veuve Cliquot, Dr. Katz recognized Mr. Victor's costar, Selena Cabot, recipient of a procedure he termed "youthenasia," a complete makeover from head to toe. She was holding up exceptionally well.

Then there was partygiver Isobel von Braun, for whom he had performed two facelifts and one throat trim. She was overdue for a second.

Elizabeth Clarke had made muted inquiries about breast reduction, by all appearances a sensible idea.

He'd given Mary Tallmadge a lift for her theatrical career, as well as removing owlish bags from beneath the eyes of Reggie Burbage. Onstage the two appeared far younger than their years.

Robin Perkins had received a tush tuck.

And he'd even been of service to the club's wealthiest member, Arthur Auchincloss. After prostate surgery the womanizing financier despaired he might never again hear cries of pleasure. However, Dr. Katz boasted to himself, I restored his confidence by sculpting the most beautiful penile implant you'll ever see.

As a Jewish bachelor, Seymour knew it was unlikely he'd ever be invited to apply for club membership, but this didn't trouble him because he wasn't at all athletic and preferred devoting time to a cherished butterfly collection. Besides, Selena Cabot graciously included him at many dinners as extra man to complete the table. Frequently this meant he was obliged to escort the enormous sculptress, Morgan Ball, but at least conversation was unrequired because the woman blathered endlessly about upbringing on a Dakota reservation where, she boomed, you were lucky to nibble on a haunch of buffalo.

Some meals, he reflected, come at cost.

Isolated, adrift in a sea of conversation, he encountered a suspicious gaze. Though guiltless, for safety's sake Seymour took refuge in the men's room.

The suspicious face was that of chief of security Ned Jarvis, ever-alert for misbehavior. Jarvis was proud that his expertise had transformed Elsinore Country Club into an impenetrable fortress: the gated entrance, fences bristling with barbed wire, every home equipped with its own alarm system, electronic beams crisscrossing rooms to deter thieves, rapists, and murderers. He'd even convinced the Board to forbid members to have pets, lest animals set off an armed response.

Jarvis disdained Loma Bella police chief Chuck Mooney as an incompetent dolt. Only in a worst-case scenario would he call for city backup.

The pair had been classmates at LAPD Academy, Mooney graduating in the top ten, Jarvis near the bottom. Both were assigned to the Loma Bella police force the same year, where they earned trademark soubriquets—"Bulldog" Jarvis for plodding efficiency, "Cuffs" Mooney for his famous blunder: he had once manacled the visiting Harlem Globetrotters, spreadeagled, face down on the sidewalk. Resigned that fate had cast him to play second fiddle, that promotion to the pinnacle was hopeless,

Bulldog took early retirement to accept the post as Elsinore's head of security. He took satisfaction in two facts: his salary exceeded what the city could afford to pay Cuffs and, though a stocky man, he was more sightly than his bald, beefy counterpart.

Jarvis's most vexing problem was the membership itself. The majority being of advanced years, a few senile, they'd either forget they'd activated the house alarm on departure, or on return would punch in the wrong code. So from dawn to closing of the clubhouse dining room, Elsinore heard more bells than a glockenspiel concert. Bulldog's force of two sedans was kept busy speeding from one hot spot to another in futile response.

The problem, raised in a Board meeting, roused spirited debate. One side was in favor of silencing the bells altogether, replacing them with a silent signal, a light on Bulldog's security screen. Opponents argued that noise is the greatest deterrent to crime, frightening away evil-doers and warning would-be victims. By a narrow margin the bells carried the day. Nevertheless, in exchange for an extra week's vacation, Jarvis was asked to monitor a light show more luminous than the White House Christmas tree.

Forget phantom criminals, he thought. The most serious threat to security comes from one of ours, Mrs. Arthur Auchincloss. The club's safest when the woman is not in residence, when she's downtown, out on a fairway, or in someone else's house.

When she's home every man and his dimwit cousin knows she likes to sunbathe in the nude. Her swimming pool is just behind a wall of shrubbery, and on Men's Day horny golfers on the ninth fairway will deliberately hook a ball as excuse for sneaking a peek. Using a club, they pretend to search for it, poking and stabbing until they trigger the alarm.

It's the same every week. The woman scrambles to get a robe

on, then sends a servant to shut the damned thing off. She's complained I should do something about it, but how am I supposed to control sex-starved philanderers? If she thinks *she's* inconvenienced, she's got nothing on me.

And now, to compound my headaches, I'm supposed to protect Mrs. von Braun's houseguest. She's asked that I post a vehicle outside Hydrangea as a twenty-four-hour deterrent, actually worried some deranged woman might be hot to tear the guy's clothes off.

Any old day. One look was all I needed to see that protection for the actor is less necessary than protection *from* him. While I was mingling incognito with the Elizabethans at the welcoming bash—a dandy disguise, by the way, a hangman with a hood over my face—I got an up-close look at Victor in action. When he wasn't guzzling booze he was checking out every pretty woman in sight, undressing her with his eyes.

This guy needs protection?

Gimme a break.

As the topper, some halfwit has cast Mooney in the musical—as a theater doorman. And word has it he's even being asked to dance! What do you bet he trips over his own feet?

As actors say—Break a leg, Cuffs.

6

AT THE FIRST music rehearsal for *Kiss Me Kate* no one was more nervous than Romero Players star Mary Tallmadge. Originally, when Reggie decided to pick up the gauntlet, accepting the challenge of musical theater, Mary considered protesting, but to do so would be to remind him he'd blundered badly once before, with the critically vilified production of *Streetcar*, and this new concept was so daring its hazards hardly required enumeration.

Instead she asked, "Will Daisy be able to afford an orchestra, darling?"

Reg was bursting his buttons. "Hardly, old hen. The setting is simply a theater, after all, so the music makes more sense emanating from a single piano. No need to bother with unions, is there? Put Libby Clarke on a bench and have her tinkle away."

That was then. An arpeggio reminded the Romero star she was presently seated in the theater's front row, sheet music in her lap, about to sing in public for the first time in her life.

Dressed in slacks and shirt with an ascot at his neck, Reggie bounced up the steps to the stage. "Right, then. Ready, my love? Ready to jump out of the plane, as it were? Frightfully brave of us all, don't you agree?" He clapped his hands briskly, then extended one in invitation.

Mary dreaded what must come next. A rehearsal veteran clad in gray sweatsuit and scuffed sneakers, holding copies of her five songs, she ascended the stairs. "Good morning, Libby," she said, hoping to sound cheerful.

At the piano Libby's hands expressed trepidation of their own. "Good morning, Mary. Do you have a preference for the song you'd like to sing first?"

Mouth dry as cotton, Mary ventured, "I suppose we should begin with 'Why Can't You Behave?'" She cleared her throat, then affected a singer's posture, the score held at arm's length, hoping trembling hands would not betray her.

The pianist played a short introduction followed by a pause. Mary then sang,

"Why can't you behave?
Oh, why—"

Her ear informed her she was off-key. She stopped and looked to Libby, who pressed the correct note.

Taking a deep breath, she made a second attempt. It was worse. Throwing the music to the floor she dissolved in tears. "It's no good!" she cried. "Forgive me, Reggie dear, but I simply can't do it. I—I'm not a singer, and even if I were, how could you expect me to do all the strenuous dancing? I'm too old," she moaned. "This is a role for a much younger woman, properly trained in musical comedy."

He stepped close. She accepted his embrace, even as she realized her tears were wetting his ascot. "You'll get it right, old thing."

"Never."

"But darling, what am I to do? A Romero production without you is unthinkable!"

Mary had prepared herself for this eventuality. Reg, she knew, would consider it bad luck if she didn't participate in some capacity.

"I'll play a small role, one that doesn't require singing or dancing."

"I'm not sure, old porridge. What role do you have in mind?"

"I'll play Ralph."

"Ralph?"

"Yes, the stage manager." He appeared lost. "Ralph can be a woman as easily as a man, can't he—she?" His mouth remained ajar. "Oh please say yes, Reggie. I'll be working with you as always, and furthermore I can pitch in by helping with makeup. Many of the UCLB cast may not know how to apply pancake and eye shadow properly, and I'll be there to teach them."

He stood ashen. "But what am I to do? Who else is there to play Bianca?"

She was also prepared for this. "Try speaking with Arthur Auchincloss. He has that beautiful young wife. Perhaps she's skilled enough."

His brow remained furrowed. "One problem, dearest. None of the Elsinore ladies will have anything to do with her. All of them are jealous, of course, but they worry about the girl's morals."

"For heaven's sake, she's *married*, Reggie. Doesn't that make her respectable?"

When she left, she saw him slumped over the piano, face in his hands.

Morning of my third day found me seated at a patio breakfast, partaking of Wong's freshly squeezed orange juice and eggs Benedict, thinking, I wonder what the chef would think if he knew my usual fare is Cheerios and coffee?

"For you, Mr. Victor," he said, offering a portable phone. I stared at it. "You just push the 'Talk' button."

I pushed. "Hello?"

"Rolf, old sausage," brayed Burbage. "Would you be interested to sit in on a few auditions I'm conducting this morning?"

Why not? It's not as if I have anything better to do. "Generous of you to offer, Reggie. I'd be delighted."

"The limo and I will collect you in an hour."

When I joined him in the back seat I saw he'd selected a directorial costume, dark slacks, sky-blue summer jacket, and of course another ascot. "There are just two roles left to be filled," he informed me, "but both are critical."

"I'm honored to be a witness."

Reggie cleared his throad loudly, a mannerism I'd learn meant he had something delicate to communicate. "Only decent to share a confidence, my boy. Fact is, your hostess Isobel doesn't get along with your leading lady Selena. A pity, but there you are. They're rivals, actually. Both filthy rich, each forever seeking to outdo the other in ostentation. Nothing to concern you, old fellow. Forewarned is forearmed as they say."

"I hear you. Thanks."

He nodded and changed the subject. "I do hope you'll be impressed with the Romero. It was my wife Daisy who discovered it, an old movie house destined for the wrecker's ball. She had it gutted, ordered the stage reconstructed, supervised the installation of backstage dressing rooms, and *voilà*."

"Was it Isobel who paid?"

From beneath unkempt eyebrows he cocked a suspicious eye. "No, Daisy did." Then he coughed delicately. "I'd best be forthcoming. It's possible you may hear malicious gossips whisper that I married her for the money. A slanderous lie, of course; we were high school sweethearts."

I was confused. "In England?"

"No, no, in Ottumwa, Iowa. We decided to elope—upset her parents dreadfully, I'm afraid—didn't approve of a chap seeking a career in the theater. Would have won them over eventually, of course, but the dears perished in an auto accident, leaving Daisy this obscene amount of money from meat packing." He paused, puzzled. "Have I said something amusing?"

"No. Forgive me." I erased the smile. I could only imagine a girl's confusion when, somewhere between Ottumwa and New York, for no plausible reason, her husband starts talking with an English accent.

I bathed in that buoyant image as the limo cruised downtown traffic, alongside buildings of uniform Spanish architecture and tiled roofs. The driver turned in behind a large white structure and braked behind a loading ramp in a parking space stenciled "Mr. Burbage."

The ersatz Brit dismounted first, jouncing in place, washing his hands in delight. "I thought I'd give you a preview, old kipper, show you the stage where you'll be making magic."

He took an elbow, intending to guide me away. I don't like strangers touching me, so I disengaged myself by pretending to look around. The whitewashed theater was yet another Spanish-style building. Across the street was a self-serve Shell station and the Mission motel, its "Vacancy" sign alight; on a diagonal corner stood the central branch post office. Dead ahead, at the edge of an expanse of grass, was a kiosk that advertised:

AUGUST 6–SEPTEMBER 4
COLE PORTER'S
KISS ME KATE

A brick walk led to twin porticoes supporting the Romero Theater. Burbage grasped an iron handle to open one of two massive oak doors, saying, "No key necessary. Visitors always welcome."

Inside, a bank of red seats sloped to a closed curtain. I paused. "What's the seating capacity?"

"Six hundred and twenty-five. A comfortable number, don't you think? And here, feel the quality. Ultrasuede." He took a whiff of pride. "Let me show you backstage."

I followed his jaunty progress down an aisle. At its base I looked around and commented, "This area's kind of small for an orchestra pit."

He stopped, wearing his astonished expression. "Orchestra?"

"Yes. How can the musicians fit in this cramped space?"

"Musicians?"

My heart took a plunge to my shoes. "Yes."

"Oh no, dear fellow. We needn't trouble with unions and all that bother, do we? The setting is a simple theater stage, after all; a single piano will do. Wait 'til you hear Libby Clarke at the ivories. She's smashing."

I vented a silent scream. Victor, you imbecile! How in hell could you have been so stupid to involve yourself in such a Mickey Mouse operation? I continued flagellating myself while Burbage checked his watch. Abruptly, he marched up an aisle,

sat down toward the rear of the orchestra, and patted the plush
seat next to him.

"First," he called, "we'll consider Lord Peter Glenn."

This was becoming more bizarre by the moment. I was shaking my head when I accepted the adjoining seat. "You're kidding me—we're auditioning a genuine lord?"

"Honestly. A Canadian lord, but his title is genuine. Vancouver Sunset, his residence, isn't far from Wilde House, my home
on Gertrude Circle. I do hope the man doesn't bollox it up, because Lady Louise is best friend of your costar, Selena Cabot;
they're tight as two ticks." He sighed. "Well, the part is Baptista,
the Shrew's father, requiring no singing or dancing, merely pa-
rental concern. Simple enough, what? Lord Peter has charisma.
Before retirement he was a hugely successful trial attorney and
has, as you might imagine, a commanding voice."

"Then what's the problem? Why not just give him the part?"

He massaged a knitted brow. "It's a believability problem,
don't you see. He's not that many years older than Selena, so
we'll have to decide if his facial structure lends itself to aging."
Again an anxious sigh. "Well, in a pinch I suppose we could glue
on a white wig."

"I see. So the second audition is his wife?"

"Oh gracious no. Lady Louise is a mousy little thing. Speaks
so rapidly and breathlessly, half the time no one can understand
what on earth she's attempting to communicate. Though she all
but disappears in her husband's shadow, it's she who has the social credentials. Lord Peter came from a family of commercial
fishermen, humble trawlers—a fact never mentioned, of course.
It was she who gave him a leg up the ladder."

Reaching into his briefcase Burbage extracted two manu-
scripts, then did a double-take. "By Jove, I believe I've neglected to give you a copy of the text. Terribly forgetful of me. Here
you are."

I laughed. "Better late than never, Reg."

"You *do* have sheet music of all the songs, I hope."

"That I have. Until now, the text I had not."

He was tsking self-reproach when a tall man, reed-thin, appeared in the aisle, wearing clothes that made his priorities clear: tan, knee-length shorts, Nikes, and a brown golf shirt with an Elsinore logo.

"Good morning to you, Lord Peter," the director said. "Frightfully sorry to have delayed your golf game. Permit me to introduce our guest star, Rolf Victor."

I stood to shake his hand. "Break a leg," I said.

He looked insulted. "What'd you say?"

I'd forgotten he was a civilian. Burbage rescued me by extending the second manuscript.

"Here we are, Lord Peter. Please take this copy with you on-stage."

The lord used stairs at the side of the proscenium to ascend, joining a piano illuminated by light from a single stanchion.

The director called, "Turn to page thirty-two, please. Take a few moments to familiarize yourself with the lines. Your character, Baptista, is a father caught between a rock and a hard place, as he says here."

"You want just the first paragraph?"

"No, all three please, but only when you're ready."

Glenn glanced briefly at the material before announcing, "Ready."

"Then begin."

BAPTISTA: Gentlemen, importune me no further,
For how I firmly am resolved you know;
That is, not to bestow my youngest daughter
Before I have a husband for the elder:
If either of you both love Katharina,

Because I know you well, and love you well,
Leave shall you have to court her at your pleasure.

Oh, if only I could find a man
That would thoroughly woo her, wed her
And bed her, and rid my house of her.

Signior Lucentio, this is the 'pointed day
That Katherine and Petruchio should be married,
And yet we hear not of our son-in-law.
What will be said? what mockery will it be,
To want the bridegroom when the priest attends
To speak the ceremonial rites of marriage!
What says Lucentio to this shame of ours?

"Am I late?" Libby Clarke whispered, resting her bosom on the back of Burbage's seat.

He shook his head. "Mrs. Auchincloss isn't due for another fifteen minutes. Relax, my love; we're almost done with Lord Peter." Then he called, "That was splendid, sir. You have a re-markably vigorous voice."

Glenn smirked. "A lifetime convincing juries of a client's in-nocence requires a voice of conviction."

"Indeed. But the difficulty here, Lord Peter, is that Baptista is a—how shall I say—a timorous man. The sort who's a hen-pecked husband, don't you know. I'd be grateful if you'd put your virility aside for a moment and instead give us your idea of a Milquetoast."

The retired lawyer laughed. "It's a stretch, but I suppose that's why they call this 'acting.'"

"Exactly right."

Glenn cleared his throat, then gave us his impression of a dweeb.

"Jolly good," said Burbage, applauding. Turning to me he said, "Once we fit him for silver hair I believe he'll make a fine Baptista. You agree?"

"Most definitely."

Burbage guffawed. "You've just been given the official stamp of approval, old prune. Congratulations and welcome to the cast."

"Sorry to run, boys," Glenn said, scurrying down the stairs and up the aisle. "Here's your script."

Reggie waved it away. "Keep it, Lord Peter. You'll be needing it for rehearsals three days hence."

"Gotta make my tee time."

"Swing smoothly," I called to his disappearing back.

He almost collided with two people simultaneously entering, a middle-aged man with a big nose and a girl at least forty years younger, an amazing blonde wearing a tight miniskirt, along with an open-necked man's shirt that exposed appetizing cleavage. This was a breathtaking surprise.

"We're early, I know," said the guy, sniffing. "But I've trained Bunny to be punctual."

"This is—?" I muttered to the director.

"Why, the second audition, of course." He rose, saying, "Welcome, welcome. Please make yourselves at home." He offered a hand, first to the knockout, then her companion. "Mr. and Mrs. Auchincloss, we met briefly at the club, but I doubt you'd remember me. I am Reginald Burbage."

"Of course we remember you," the husband said, and sniffed.

"This is our visiting guest star, Mr. Rolf Victor." I shook hands, averting my eyes from the overflowing treats. "And this lady is our musical director, Libby Clarke."

More handshakes, then an awkward silence as everybody stood around wondering what came next.

At last Reggie clapped his hands together. "As Rolf has learned, I'm a firm believer in candor. My original choice for the role of Bianca was my long-standing leading lady, Mary Tallmadge, but she rejected it, nattering about how she lacked musical comedy skills. Broke my heart, really, but now I must concede she may have been a tad—mature for the role. You, Mrs. Auchincloss, assuredly possess the intended appearance."

The nerd took another intake of air through his beaked nose, a mannerism that said, I have money to buy and sell jerks like you, and as for my wife, eat your hearts out. It also said he knew women found him irresistible, and who's to say he wasn't?

"Well—" Reggie exhaled. "Without further ado, the stage is yours, Mrs. Auchincloss. To be shared with Libby, of course."

The pianist was clutching the score to her bosom. "Which number have you chosen, ma'am?"

"Call her Bunny," the snob said. "She wants to do 'Always True To You In My Fashion.'"

Bunny nodded and followed Libby in ascending the stairs. She had yet to speak. There was a subdued sadness about her that made me guess that, though she looked perfect for the part, she'd lack pizzazz.

The pianist set out the music, made herself comfortable on the stool, then looked to where the singer was leaning against the piano. At her nod Libby played the intro.

Bunny sang softly, plaintively, a pretty voice in a beautiful package, nice but nothing special. Until she hit the segue into Porter's raunchy lyrics, when she transformed herself into an uninhibited sexpot. She began by flinging out an uncovered leg, teasing us, promising we were in for something, then she spun, leaped, and tapped to the perimeters of the stage, her hands sometimes expressing innocence, sometimes lust, her voice alternately brassy and subdued, alternately shy and sluttish. At the climax she made love to the stanchion.

At the closing chord I saw old Reggie's mouth ajar, a man resurrected from the dead, entertaining thoughts he believed long-buried.

I glanced over at Auchincloss and, yes, he was right—I was eating my heart out. "What do you think, Burbage?" asked the jerk.

The director swallowed. "Well, I had no idea—" he began, and swallowed again.

"Does she get the part?"

"My gracious, I—"

"Velvet's your choreographer, right? Velvet Jackson?"

"Yes."

"She and Bunny work well together. You'll be happy." He stood and slapped Reggie on the shoulder. "C'mon, puss," he called. "Time to bye-bye."

Arthur Auchincloss liked to reflect on how his life had changed since Portland. I didn't mind losing the mansion, even the vineyard in France—I'd have given anything to get rid of the vindictive bitch.

I got bushwhacked because I just wasn't paying attention. She wanted children; I didn't. So she wanted to go back to college; no problem. Wanted to enroll in law school; okay, good luck.

I once yawned, "Are you specializing in any specific field?"

Only being polite, of course, but I should have listened to her answer. "Yes. Divorce law."

My housekeeper Zena was right on when she said, "Guid rrridance, sirrr." The Scot's been a helluva lot more loyal than my two wives and eleven live-ins, never judgmental, never sharing thoughts that must simmer beneath her silver bun.

Heck, she didn't even open her peep when, as a gag, I gave a bash inviting every woman in the Pacific Northwest I'd had sex with—without their husbands, natch. Well, it was a nice turn-out, twenty-six in all, but the jig was up when they finally guessed what they had in common. Half stormed out, while the other half sat around, got drunk, and lied about what a lousy lay I am.

Anyhow, once construction was completed, Zena and I moved into Bulls and Bears, off Elsinore's ninth fairway. People figured a bachelor must be lonely, but not me. I got invited out a lot as extra man at dinner parties, and I was popular because I was generous with investment advice. For instance, I increased Isobel von Braun's portfolio by six percent.

"I'm taking off for Sun Valley," I alerted her. "Gotta get in some skiing."

At least that's what I intended to do. But snow was farthest from my mind once I entered the Lodge gift shop. Bam! There she was, the girl of my dreams, so drop-dead gorgeous I stood zapped in my tracks. It took me minutes to unglue my lips to make her acquaintance.

"I'm getting married," I phoned Isobel.

"You've only been gone two days, dear," she chided.

"This is the person I intend to spend the rest of my life with. She's a little younger than I am—" All right, so I neglected to say by forty-four years—"but she's so good for me. Can you make the wedding?"

"Ah, just when is it to be, Arthur?"

"Saturday. We're taking our vows on a lift to the summit of Snake Mountain. My instructor, Hans, and Bunny's boss, Wil-ma, will be witnesses in the chair below. From above Padre Paul of the Minutemen will read scripture. It'll be a hoot. Can I save you a T-bar?"

Isobel expelled that hissing laugh. "You wicked scamp, tempting an old woman."

And the rest is history.

However, a guy doesn't amass a few billion without anticipat-
ing where the market's headed, and I worried Bunny might
have eyes for younger guys. Shame on me. It's no accident she
calls me Daddy because that's what I am, a father figure, somebody to replace the bastard who ditched her family in Pocatello,
Idaho. She needed a provider, someone to care for her in every
way, and that's me. No, it'd never occur to her to cheat on somebody who provides her with love and kindness because there
isn't a mean bone in Bunny's body. She's a little dim, maybe, but
genuinely sweet.

True, she likes dressing in tight miniskirts and is proud of her
cleavage, as she should be, and believe me, *I'm* proud to be the
guy who tucks her in at night. I'd be lying if I said I didn't get a
kick out of the double-takes she causes; I saw one lech walk
smack into a light pole.

But eventually it got me to thinking she should have some
kind of life other than wasting every afternoon watching those
crappy soaps. Hell, with her looks, she could have some kind of
career in show business where people would pay to see her.

"You ever done any singing, puss?" I asked during a commercial.

"No."

"Dancing?"

"Only with you."

"Would you be interested in learning?"

She shrugged, distracted again by the actress with amnesia.

So I asked around to find somebody qualified to teach Bunny
and was directed to a Loma Bella night club called Velvet's. It
turns out Velvet herself was a famous dancer who got her start
in Harlem's Cotton Club before kicking up her heels on Broadway.

She had no interest in taking on Bunny until I named a sum
that opened her chocolate eyes.

"Can you recommend somebody to give her singing lessons?" I asked.

And she picked up a phone that got us an interview with Conrad Summers, the guy who trained a number of people who went on to sing leads in Broadway shows.

So we set up a schedule: Velvet works with Bunny from nine to noon, coaching her in free form and tap. An hour off for lunch, two hours for the crappy soaps, then Conrad takes over at the piano from three to six, demonstrating breathing and voice placement.

I have time to down three stiff pops, Zena has dinner on the table at seven, and Daddy's bedtime is ten. Okay, a few times a week incest is involved, but Bunny doesn't seem to mind. In fact, her lessons have given her so much pep she's first in bed.

Both teachers are enthusiastic, and not just about their salaries. They say my wife's a natural, and it's reached a point where I can see and hear that myself. So Puss and I have a life, which is more than I can say for certain people. I'm talking about air-heads who waste hours arguing over who's nastier—my pal Isobel or her nemesis Selena Cabot.

7

ONE SHORT YEAR prior to Isobel making her commitment to *Kiss Me Kate*, she and Selena were navigating turbulent waters that threatened to drown their closest friends. The storm arose during an accidental disclosure.

On an unbearably hot day Mary Clarke (as she was known then) decided she was in no mood for her hair appointment. She called to cancel it and drove from town to Bowflex with the intention of enjoying a cold shower.

Her thoughts were focused on Baxter, because recent encounters with friends had turned awkward, conversations curtailed at her appearance, along with sorrowful countenances, even expressions of pity. These signals, she'd heard, were indications of an unfaithful husband.

But that's nonsense, she thought. My husband's never given me cause for suspicion. He continues to desire me; why, two or three times a week he pinches my buttocks as warning I'm about to be swept up and taken to bed.

"You're all the woman I'll ever need," he likes to say.

Of course, people assume I married Baxter because I was attracted by his physique. Superficially this is so, I suppose, but more importantly I was drawn to him by the reason he'd sculpted it. He confided he'd been bullied horribly as a boy, and resolved to create an antidote to cruelty.

No woman of sensitivity could fail to be touched by that, and Romero audiences will tell you Sensitivity is my middle name.

No, I'm just being foolish, she rebuked herself, opening the wardrobe closet to choose the orange terrycloth robe. She was but dimly aware the bathroom door was closed. Then, when she opened it, to her shock and dismay, she saw the shower already occupied—by her husband, soaping the body of that scarecrow Meredythe Kister.

The murmurs of secret dialogues amplified to a sudden roar. "Baxter Clarke is unfaithful to his wife and she's so dim she doesn't see!"

Standing rooted on the bathroom tile, blindfold lifted at last, Mary cried aloud, "Enough!"

Octogenarian Horace Tallmadge, a retired Judge, lived five doors down from Bowflex. His home, Sidebar, was also on Polonius Place.

He thought, I remember when Mary Clarke called asking if

I might recommend a good divorce attorney I didn't hesitate. "Simon Sharp," I said.

It never occurred to me at the time that she might be asking for herself. I wondered later if I'd heard correctly because these damned hearing aids are always cutting up and lately I've noticed I've become more forgetful.

I know I didn't mention the call to my better half because Libby wakened me from my nap, in a tizzy about the breakup at Bowflex. Being so much younger than I am, she tends to get excited.

Not in the bedtime way, because when we courted I told her flat out, I'm a widower. Those fires were doused long ago.

She said that was okay, those matters no longer interested her either. She has this complex about her looks—she's a round little thing with a bosom that makes her stoop-shouldered.

But I owe her everything. She inherited a fortune from Arco oil, and if it weren't for her money I'd never have been able to buy the beautiful home or join this club because all I had was a skimpy judicial pension.

To those who wonder (never aloud, of course) what in the world she saw in me, I mention we met at a chess class. I got her attention by mating her in fourteen moves.

Too bad about the Clarkes. I'm proud to say the Tallmadge marriage is rock-solid.

Baxter Clarke wasn't licking his wounds over Mary's defection. The divorce was going to cost him, no question, but he had plenty left from the sale of his father's Madison Avenue publishing company.

What rankled most was Mary making such a to-do about infidelity. So what's the big deal? It doesn't mean anything. Look, some nights a man's in the mood for chicken, right? Next night he's hungry for steak, another night he wants turkey, or ham, or pizza or whatever.

It's ridiculous. Well, you won't see Baxter Clarke living alone for long, and I believe I know just the woman to help me get over my loss. It's common knowledge Libby Tallmadge is richest of all the Elsinore heiresses, and she can't be gettin' a whole lot of lovin' from the geezer.

How could I have been so blind? Mary Clarke asked herself yet again. The Bekins movers had left all her belongings as islands on the carpet of her rented one-bedroom downtown apartment. She was still too upset to unpack, so the ringing telephone was no intrusion.

"Hello?"

The voice was feeble but agitated. "Mary, this Horace—Horace Tallmadge?"

"Hello, Judge."

"By any chance is my wife—is Libby visiting you?"

"No, she's not here. Why?"

"Well, I was taking a nap," he said breathily. "Woke up. Looked everywhere, but she was gone; just vanished. So I've been calling people, hoping—"

A sudden flash of lightning illumined Mary's mind. He wouldn't, she thought, and then, Oh yes, he would. "Horace," she said, "let me make some inquiries. In the meantime, please do your best to remain calm."

When Baxter answered her call she said, "You've got her, haven't you, you scoundrel."

"Who? Oh—you mean you want to talk to Libby?"

And the fugitive's voice came on, bubbling with achievement. "Mary, I've never been so happy!"

"Have you no shame?"

"It's just that Baxter believes I'm incredibly sexy. Can you imagine?"

What a dire sequence of events! Mary thought, just who is going to look after the ancient judge? Someone must. Myself?

Well, I have nothing to offer but sympathy, and I have plenty of that, so I'll help by visiting once a day.

And so I did, brewing a pot of tea for the stunned man, smoothing his remaining wisps of hair, sympathizing over the injustice that baffled him so.

Inevitably, just a week later, Horace quavered, "You're such a good person, Mary; you'd never desert an old man. I'm so lonely and so crave company. Would you—could you—consider becoming my wife?"

I patted his hand, thinking, You've always made such a crusade of caring for the handicapped, Mary, and it isn't as if you'd have to tend to him physically—he has a live-in nurse to do that—

"It wouldn't work, Horace. Though I have little to do in *Kiss Me Kate*, you may remember normally I'm extremely busy acting in Romero productions. I'm always either in rehearsal or performing. I can't wait to get back into harness."

The sweet man must have had his hearing aids turned off because he gushed, "Oh, I'll be so proud!"

And so it came to pass that Mary Clarke (now Tallmadge) moved her downtown belongings into Sidebar, while Libby Tallmadge (now Clarke) filled the doorways at Bowflex.

8

THE DIZZYING sequence of events celebrated as "The Swap Meet" might have been no more than a passing gust of Santa Ana wind, had Selena let the affairs die there. But the phone line from Versailles sizzled with scorching criticism of Baxter Clarke, the man Frederick von Braun had proclaimed his dearest friend, thereby fanning a conflagration of hostilities.

That this wedge was being driven between the two principal contributors to *Kiss Me Kate*—Isobel financially, Selena artistically—was upsetting to many, especially because differences were not being settled discreetly, behind closed doors.

Isobel deliberately chose a public place to fire the opening salvo when she accosted Selena at bridge. "Are you beyond remorse?" she hissed, shoulders swollen, head drawn back, tongue flicking. "How dare you spread malicious lies! How dare you insinuate Baxter Clarke is guilty of adulterous improprieties!"

Selena calmly considered her hand. "I insinuate nothing that isn't common knowledge, darling. It's no affair of mine that your Baxter wears a bikini the size of a postage stamp. My quarrel with him is that, small as it is, he can't keep it on."

Isobel gasped, but her retort did the rounds of Loma Bella luncheons for months. Smiling venomously, she said, "Only a former chorine could think that remark amusing, dear. I'm sure during your singing and dancing days you *always* spurned stage door Johnnies."

Selena's response was also quoted extensively. "My reputation was impeccable, sweet Isobel. Surely the private detective you hired to investigate my past has told you as much."

Isobel feigned shock. "Private detective? You believe I'd sink so low, that I'd resort to such an underhanded stratagem? You forget, dear, I am a respected parishioner at Saint Cecilia."

Selena nodded. "The clerics must worship you, love; or rather, your money. You're a tither, I believe."

Isobel's mouth set in smug superiority. "You've been informed accurately. It's a pity you won't join us of a Sunday."

"Saint Isobel, the day you see me seated in a pew will be the day Baxter Clarke becomes a Franciscan monk."

With that, the battle lines were drawn. Ever after the two women were cordial in public and, when necessary, even falsely affectionate. But communal interests notwithstanding, the air at Elsinore remained tainted by contentious pollution.

There being no place to hide, innocent ladies were caught in the crossfire. Lady Louise, of course, sided with close friend Selena, yet felt she owed an explanation to her husband.

She broached the subject at breakfast, while he was reading the morning *Sun*. "Despite her impressive wealth, dear, there is a coarse side to Isobel von Braun that is difficult to describe. The way she dresses, for example—carelessly, dowdily, card room apparel. While Selena Cabot is always dressed elegantly and tastefully, as if prepared to pour high tea."

"Mm."

Well, I bore him as usual, she thought. Or perhaps I'm speaking too rapidly for him to appreciate the importance of what I'm alluding to.

"You see, Peter, in this enduring conflict we must choose one side or the other—either Isobel's clique, the 'Sensible People,' or Selena's coterie of 'Bohemians.'"

"Mm."

"Take, for example, the difference between the two women's hands. Selena has lovely hands—the slender fingers, the nails immaculately manicured—while von Braun's hands are thick, almost—how shall I say it? Yes, almost—pugilistic."

"Mm."

"And I remind you that you've always enjoyed the arts, dear—theater, painting, sculpture and the like. And now here you are, performing every night on the stage! So what do you say, my thespian? I vote we become Bohemians!"

Kip Perkins was a Sensible Person only by association, but today behaved more like a Bohemian, humming a melody from the show, "Wunderbar," as he waltzed around his room, guiding an imaginary partner, feet kissing the carpet.

It was Sunday, a full day off from rehearsals. It meant the

afternoon was his, to drive the Fairlane down to Surfland Road, park and lock it, cross the railroad tracks to a path that led down to Paradise Beach, there to be welcomed by fellow nudists.

Many envied his tan, wondering how any man who worked for a living could maintain it. Little did they know that at every opportunity he was sunning himself beside Hydrangea's swimming pool.

As he undressed he arranged his clothing fastidiously on a pink towel spread on the sand, then inhaled invigorating ocean air while observing the crowd. There were more hunks than usual, some of them strangers, perhaps visitors from Los Angeles. Yes indeedy, word's getting out about my beloved beach!

He sang aloud, "Take my hand, I'm a stranger in paradise!"

He basked in giggles and applause, even from the cows and sows. He waved appreciation, then pranced to the ocean's edge and stood in water up to his ankles, bending to cup handfuls of water and splash them on his torso, aware that eyes of the butch brigade were devouring his taut buttocks.

Shame, shame, Kippy. How you love to tantalize!

Tut! I can tease all I like, because once through the gates of Elsinore, I'm free as a—yes, free as a Robin.

Ah, tonight should be smashing, he mused. It's really my calling, presiding at the head of Table One, orchestrating the conversation, making each and every guest feel important. And when it comes time to trip the light fantastic—well, I'm more than the best ballroom dancer in Elsinore, I'm uncrowned champion of Loma Bella. How many other men know the lyrics to every song Cole Porter ever wrote, including all the verses? How many do such a perfect impression of Judy Garland it gives people goosebumps?

"Your social graces are unmatched," Snookums likes to say, reaching to pinch my cheek between a thumb and forefinger. "You charmer."

It makes me shiver with pleasure.

Though my official title is "fiancé," we both understand marriage is never intended. Like a stray puppy, at age thirty-eight, I wandered down the right driveway at the right time. It was kismet. I'd just been dumped by that traitor, Earl. I was experienced at bathing and wiping old bottoms at Eisenhower hospital in the desert, and a nurse at Mercy referred me to a Frederick von Braun.

Yes, kismet!

It's true I find the disapproval of the club's male membership disappointing. But I can handle rejection; I'm accustomed to it. Even the temperamental Wong disapproves of me, can you imagine? An oriental who's probably a communist spy, who treats me like I'm a fellow servant, interrupting social responsibilities to demand immediate assistance!

Ah, thank God for my sanctuary, my precious room with its own TV. I get to watch or tape all the soap operas; I get to weep all I want without shame.

How many people my age can say they live on a generous allowance in return for being an occasional chauffeur, otherwise hired just to be fun and pretty?

Which reminds me. A visiting fireman with an impressive hose has been ogling me.

Picking up my tube of sun block, I skipped over and offered it, saying, "Be an angel, sailor? Rub this on my back?"

Ashley Faye was puzzled to receive a telephone call from a man she knew only by reputation, Romero artistic director Reggie Burbage. "Lovely woman, my box office staff has resigned, just upped and quit, babbling rubbish about early retirement. This at a time when we're being inundated with requests for *Kiss Me Kate*. The cheek! Now I am without two indispensable people to sell tickets and assign seats. You come highly recommended to me by Selena Cabot, who proclaims you the most responsible person in all of Loma Bella."

That's how it started, Ashley remembered. Despite the work-load I have at Saint Cecilia—marriage counselor and head of the Altar Guild—I allowed a stranger to sweet-talk me into accepting another challenge. How is it possible I agreed to take this on, considering Saint Cecilia is my life?

I mean, I was married at the church originally, long before the Lord called me, but my later vows were taken less conspicuously, once at the Loma Bella courthouse, another time in Las Vegas, later in an Oxnard chapel, and to Trevor in a gazebo overlooking the Pacific at Pismo Beach.

Trevor's the first husband capable of actually supporting me. My previous exes were, respectively, an Amana salesman, a lifeguard, an auto mechanic, and a tennis pro.

To demonstrate his commitment, Trevor became a docile regular at Sunday's eleven o'clock service—until I changed my mind, aware that his alcoholic fumes emptied the pew. So I told him, "Just rest at home, darling, and leave the Lord to me."

Of course, no one noticed his absence, leaving me free to perform cheerful service. It's been said no one can ever recall having seen Ashley Faye when she wasn't wearing a smile, an observation I esteem as a singular compliment.

I admit it took time for me to come to the truth. I'm mortified to recall that during my years at Loma Bella High I had the reputation of being promiscuous, and as a younger woman I also experimented with any number of self-help philosophies. I was, in turn, a confirmed Buddhist, Scientologist, est-ian, evangelical, Muslim, and Zoroastrian.

But all that changed after I met blessed Isobel von Braun. I owe everything to her. It was Isobel who awakened my soul with a simple request, that I join her at a Saint Cecilia eleven o'clock service, seating me deliberately in the front pew.

When Reverend Kenneth Holly stepped to the pulpit to announce the opening hymn, I was breathtaken—a man in his early thirties, tall and broad-shouldered, wearing designer spectacles, a holy presence whose sonorous voice filled the church.

When it came time for communion, I longed to partake, if only to be served by him, but as a guest it wasn't my privilege. So I remained seated as Isobel rose to hiss, "Watch my purse."

Shaking the reverend's hand afterward, I felt the clasp of the Lord and never let go, unqualifiedly accepting Him into my life.

"Why oh why, Isobel dear, didn't you bring me sooner?" I groaned.

Months later, when my duties as marriage counselor brought me daily conference with Reverend Holly, I became dismayed to detect tiny imperfections, like chips in a stained glass window.

His scheme to import a choir from the African Pentecostal Church in Watts had a lofty purpose, but proved mistaken. As the visiting choristers sang, shouted, and clapped hands, infused with the holy spirit, Saint Cecilia regulars sat like monuments in a graveyard; subsequent mingling in the courtyard proved an interracial ordeal.

Yet the reverend expressed gratitude. "The church needs a woman like you, Ashley," he said. "Somebody willing to experiment, somebody to bring Saint Cecilia into the twenty-first century."

Then he invited me to join him for a few days' retreat at a mountain monastery. Ah, the peace! Just praying and fasting, and a perplexing ritual he described as "the laying on of hands." Examining myself later, feeling the places he'd touched me, where, I asked, were the miraculous results?

But what upset me most was the healer's expression when he addressed the youth group. Was it my imagination that "Rev Ken" seemed to single out only the prettiest girls for counseling? Or was this but another indication the devil was at work, challenging my faith?

The Lord provided an answer following a youth excursion to

the Sierras, when Beatrice Hester appeared in my office with a shocking charge—Reverend Holly had crawled into the sleeping bag of sixteen-year-old Samantha Leslie!

"It was okay with Sam," said Beatrice, "but the rest of us didn't get much sleep."

Outraged, I confronted the cad at once, demanding an explanation, but he appeared more outraged than I, deeming the accusation slanderous, denying it so vehemently I retreated. Months later he was still denying it, despite evidence Samantha was pregnant.

Reverend Kenneth Holly's closing words as shepherd of Saint Cecilia's flock were, "I don't have the money to pay for an abortion."

So quietly I went about raising the necessary funds from parishioners like Isobel, swearing them to secrecy. But I should have guessed the scandal would inevitably reach unsympathetic ears. The jackals feasted.

I was Isobel's dinner guest when predator Selena Cabot approached our table. "Izzie," she began, using an abhorred nickname, "how perfectly shocking and humiliating all this must be! Surely neither you nor Ashley played any part in choosing a rapist to give divine instruction. Of course not. But I do worry, as a conservative like yourselves, that there are those in your congregation who appear pro-choice. Could you enlighten me, dear ones? I'm at sea."

Deciding it wisest to drop out of sight for a time, I informed Trevor we wouldn't be dining at the club for the present because I was too busy leading a search committee to find Holly's replacement.

My spouse's sole comment on the affair was snide. "Didn't you tell me he graduated from Harvard Inseminary?"

I set rigid ground rules for my quest. If a candidate was an attractive man of any age, he was rejected out of hand. The remainder received precise examination; applicants admitting to a fondness for soul music or love of the outdoors were erased on the spot.

Ultimately, after consultation with tither von Braun, I approved the choice of Reverend Jeremiah Drain, a pastor in his late fifties, who in all likelihood hadn't forced himself on the skittish Mrs. Drain for decades. His sermons were thoughtful, if not thought-provoking, delivered in a nasal monotone that worsened at onset of the olive blossoms, when he clutched the Bible in one hand, a handkerchief in the other, wiping away fluids from his dripping sinuses.

The Cabot woman struck again, approaching Table One where Isobel, Kip, Trevor, and I were complaining about choices at the buffet. "Congratulations to you all! I'm told Saint Cecilia was well attended Sunday last, and that thanks to a splendid antihistamine, your minister is now dripping with charm. Selfish things, don't keep him and Mrs. Drain all to yourselves. You must host a party to introduce them to your less spiritual friends."

I refuse to be daunted. My enthusiasm remains intact. Each Sunday, following the service, I circulate in the courtyard among the congregation, distributing my accustomed cheer, asking, "Weren't the reverend's words utterly inspiring?"

I can be certain Gordon and Martha Leslie, sullen Samantha sandwiched between them, will nod.

9

AS HE MOUNTED stairs to the Romero stage, director Reggie Burbage observed with satisfaction that his stage manager had fulfilled every request. There was a square table with exactly fifteen camp chairs, including his at the head, and fifteen copies of the script, ballpoint pens neatly placed on the covers. Nearby were eight haphazard chairs for the technical directors. A stanchion illuminated the piano for Libby.

When the S.M.—what was his name?—approached, I complimented him. "Deucedly efficient, old man. Done like a professional." The chap was youngish, perhaps mid-thirties, and wore designer spectacles. "Forgive me—I've forgotten your name."

"Kenneth Holly."

"Of course. And what exactly is it you do for a living?"

"I'm a chiropractor. You can find me in the Yellow Pages—under 'Magic Hands'."

"Let's see if our cast matches your professionalism." I consulted my Cartier wristwatch. "They're due in fifteen minutes."

Just then Selena Cabot entered the auditorium.

"Ah! I should have guessed you'd be leading the parade, Selena. Good show."

The door had no sooner closed than it opened again, this time admitting Bunny Auchincloss with her husband.

"Ah! Two more conscientious actors, reporting ahead of time."

As they advanced down the aisle Arthur said, "You can always count on us, Burbage." He was dressed in slacks and button-down shirt. I was relieved to see his wife had chosen an unremarkable jogging outfit.

"Please join us onstage."

Next to appear through the oak doors was Rolf Victor, together with Kip Perkins.

"Splendid. A director is fortunate to have such a punctual company."

"Rolf and I are a team, Reggie," Kip said. "I'm his wheels."

"Come—all of you come take a chair." As they were seating

themselves I observed my guest star hadn't shaved. "Dare I hope, Rolf, that I am seeing the beginning of a goatee?"

"Yup. I figure a goatee's an all-purpose look—it works for both contemporary scenes and period."

"Bully."

Selena quipped, "If it's all the same to you, Reg, I'll play this clean-shaven." After my chuckle she went on, "Since this is to be a reading, what say I move and sit across from Rolf?"

"Capital idea."

At the appointed reporting time, actors and technicians seated in the camp chairs, Libby on the piano stool, Reggie rose. Washing his hands excitedly, he said, "Well, here we all are, taking on the challenge of staging the very first musical in Romero history. Exhilarating, what?"

Addressing murmurs and tentative smiles, he continued, "This is what I propose we do today. We read the text, pausing only to hear Libby play Mr. Porter's numbers. No need for singing just yet. No. We merely want to get a feel, as it were, for the entertainment. Before we commence—Questions?"

Kip held up a hand. "Reggie, I'm a bit concerned about the dancing I'm asked to do. After all, the character's described as being a 'Broadway hoofer.' The singing's no problem, of course—"

"You have two experts to show you, old onion." The actor looked nonplussed. "But—you mean to tell me you haven't been introduced yet? Dear me." Indicating, Reggie said, "Meet Tad Wismer and Chauncey Slater, both dance majors at the University of California, Loma Bella."

An exchange of handshakes and sibilance.

"And the fellow in the end seat is Perry Nelson, who has the very athletic assignment of 'Too Darn Hot'."

The man waved, responding in a hearty voice, "Hi. I'm a theater major at UCLB who also happens to dance a little."

"You're far too modest, old muffin. More questions?"

Rolf held up a hand. "Shouldn't the members of the chorus be here, too?"

"Chorus?"

"Yes. The script says there are twenty-six singers and dancers to back up the principals."

"Twenty-six? Oh no no, dear boy, that's many too many. We don't want people crashing into one another, do we? No, I've culled the cream of talent from our outstanding university, and our marvelous choreographer will supply the rest. Am I correct, Velvet?"

The mulatto answered, "I'm training twelve."

"Perfect."

Velvet Jackson was enjoying a secret laugh. Everybody pats me on the back and tells me how generous I am for doing this out of the goodness of my heart. Any old day.

No way would I get involved with a bunch of lead-footed amateurs if Arthur Auchincloss weren't paying under the table; he's worried his wife'll look bad unless other dancers are at least acceptable. One sure as hell isn't; this Robin Perkins has rhythm only. It's up to me to teach him a passable quickstep, shuffle, and basic tap, then surround him with enough movement that audiences might not notice he's faking it. The two UCLB male dancers are okay. My students who've agreed to be in the chorus are better. Perkins is no singer, either, but that's not my department.

Selena Cabot spoke up. "If you have any more surprises, Reg, 'fess up now."

Reggie coughed. "Well. Well, I've made a few cuts here and there, nothing important."

"Like what?" said Selena.

"Well—like the entr'acte numbers, for example. We don't really need them, do we? Prolongs the show unnecessarily, and it's too long as it is."

Baxter Clarke sat up. "Hold it. Just a sec. How in hell are Hugh and I supposed to get changed from Gangster suits to tights? That takes time, a whole lot of it."

Reggie hadn't reckoned on that. "Oh, dear. My. Let me make a note here. Perhaps, Velvet, you can choreograph a dance of the period, a pavanne of some sort? A stately procession easy to learn yet time-consuming?" The choreographer sat covering her face as the director wrote on his script cover. "As for the other changes, you'll learn about them during rehearsal. Any further questions? No? So!" Reggie seated himself, opening a script with notations in varicolored ink. "Libby, old budgie, an introduction if you please, then on to 'Another Op'nin', Another Show'."

The tiny hands on the keys created clamorous sounds, crashing chords, and a heavy foot on the pedal, culminating in a crescendo followed by silence. Everyone at the table turned to look at Rolf Victor.

As Fred Graham, the actor raised his strong voice. "All right, company! Thank you!" And continuing the Spewak dialogue, he began staging curtain calls in this Baltimore tryout. Graham's ego filled the theater, challenged by the temperament of movie actress Lilli Vanessi, a belligerent Selena Cabot.

Listening, Reggie Burbage was awed. It never failed to excite him, this transformation of lettering on a printed page to the flesh, blood, and emotion of live performance. He was immersed completely, transfigured to his youth, again a youngster whose very life was bounded by the trappings of make-believe.

Selena scolded herself. I've used this theater commitment as excuse long enough. There are social obligations to be fulfilled, and out of guilt I should include my brother. When I called to include him at the table he replied, "Dinner? I dunno—Who else will be there?," as if it mattered. Hugh likes to play hard to get, though we both know he always welcomes a free meal and social attention.

"Well, I must include my closest friend, Lady Louise Glenn, with her husband Lord Peter—you remember playing golf with him—and my charming director, Reggie Burbage with his wife Daisy, and it would be nice to invite Judge Tallmadge with his new wife, Mary—she's the long-time star of the Romero players—along with the brilliant sculptress Morgan Ball." This last was risky, so I added, "She thinks you're the handsomest creature in all of Loma Bella."

"Um."

Hugh pretended to ponder, running down the cast of characters. Conversation with hummingbird Lady Glenn is always an ordeal, he thought; the woman makes no sense, talking in breathy bursts. Lord Peter, who has the balls to list himself as such in the phone book, is a loud snob who lowers his handicap by conceding himself all putts within six feet.

Reggie Burbage is the Loma Bella matinee idol, a ham actor with a British accent everyone knows is phony—people in Ottuma, Iowa, don't talk that way, especially his wife Daisy, heiress to all that meat packing money. She's too rich to bother putting on airs, so her flat midwest accent, dropping final 'g's all over the place, is enough to make you cringe.

Morgan Ball goes about six-two in her stockinged feet, dresses in Cherokee costumes, and is, of course, a bull dyke who talks louder than Lord Peter. She's also set designer for our show. At least, as her "date," I can forget conversation and concentrate on the gourmet platters dished up by Selena's chef, Jewel.

No, the person who makes this invitation tempting is Mary Tallmadge, formerly married to a muscle-bound oil slick. Though Mary's at least five years older than I am, she's a turn-on. Her British accent is for real, having been raised in— Bournemouth, is it? She mostly wears long skirts or slacks, so her legs probably aren't good, but the rest of her is dynamite— sensuous mouth and sparkling eyes framed by pageboy russet hair. From the night I first saw her onstage, her throaty magnetism had me hooked.

And now she's grafted to a fossil who probably can't remember where he last left his dentures. For sure, something's missing from Mary Tallmadge's life, and guess who has just the plug to fit in her socket?

Stifling a yawn, Hugh answered, "This Saturday, you say? Well, I suppose…"

Kiss Me Kate was Hugh Tisdale's second acting appearance, the first being his performance as Mitch in the Romero production of *A Streetcar Named Desire*. Reggie Burbage had cast Hugh for having an insouciant Ivy League demeanor that blended believably with his own invincible poise. Scenes intended by the author to express lower-class loutishness assumed the formality of a ceremony honoring the Queen's birthday.

There were those, in fact, who preferred Hugh's interpretation of Mitch to that of Karl Malden, finding it less coarse, and voiced hope he might continue his Loma Bella acting career.

These were innocents ignorant of Tisdale's odious purpose, the seduction of Blanche DuBois. Two weeks into rehearsal Mary Tallmadge still interpreted requests to run lines as the anxiety of an insecure amateur. Further, she interpreted gropes behind the scenery to be merely a clumsy tribute to her talent; so she unpinned these embraces and thrust the man away with trills of laughter. Had she not been so near-sighted and too vain to wear glasses, she might have been frightened to recognize naked lechery.

But she could hear, and at last the sounds of heavy breathing began to alarm her. Rolling up her script, she fetched Hugh a playful clout, opening a paper cut on the bridge of his nose that proved immune to styptic pencil. Seymour Katz closed it later with two stitches, but thereafter the swain was careful to remain out of Mary's reach.

Only later, during dress rehearsals, did he summon courage to renew his courtship. In lieu of physical contact, he voiced his desire in hoarse whispers. "I adore you, Mary," he croaked.

This time her script was used to fan herself. "Hugh, darling, you mustn't. I am a married woman."

"Listen—we can stash the Judge in the health unit at Casa Feliz, while you and I continue leading productive lives. I'm just the man to make you ecstatically happy."

"I could never leave Judge Horace. Speak no more."

He inched closer. "You're tempted, aren't you, woman? Come on—admit it."

"Never. Kindly desist."

"Then how's about a kiss? Where's the harm in a kiss?"

At such close range his demented eyes were terrifying. Placing both hands on Hugh's chest, Mary pushed him away, too forcibly she realized, because he lost his balance and crashed into a lighting stanchion, suffering a blow to the back of his head that required another phone call to Doctor Katz.

Mary was upset. "Why do you persist so?" she asked.

"Fair question," he said, fingering his latest bandage. "It's just that—I feel a powerful sexual attraction to you."

She frowned and emitted a deep sigh. "Oh Hugh, Hugh darling, it's the material, don't you see? It's an occupational hazard; eventually what is fiction becomes mistaken reality. You aren't in love with me, dear. You're in love with Blanche DuBois."

He ground his teeth in frustration. "Blanche or Mary, I'm dying to get you in bed."

She laughed and called across the stage, "Reggie, this boy says he wants to get me in bed. Isn't that sweet?"

"Jolly charming! Perhaps we should exchange roles here, Hughie, old leek. You strip to your vest and breathe fire on Blanche, whilst I practice restraint as Mitch."

That terminated Hugh Tisdale's efforts at seduction. He played out the remainder of the engagement in such truculent silence Mary Tallmadge eventually guessed the reason. "Ah Hugh, *now* I know why you were wooing me."

His moue demonstrated indescribable hurt.

"You wanted to marry me for the money, didn't you?"

Hugh glanced around nervously, signaling she should lower her voice. "Of course not. What an awful thing to say."

Her musical laughter cascaded two octaves. Gasping, she said, "But there *is* no money, darling. None. Apart from the Judge's pension, I haven't a bean. You'd best lift your leg on another tree."

Isobel von Braun knew that Selena's disreputable brother, Hugh Tisdale, had had an affair with a married checker at Safeway, but under terms of their pact refrained from broadcasting it.

Yet, she thought, womanizing is so mild a charge it might only disappoint aspirations for a locker at Elsinore. Little did I guess this was but one in a dossier of delicious discoveries.

On a recent afternoon, observing play through binoculars, I recognized Hugh deep in the rough off the eighteenth fairway. Glancing to be sure his opponents weren't watching, he furtively kicked his ball back onto grass.

Interesting, I thought. Do you suppose he has flaws other than womanizing and cheating? Opening my address book, I looked under "N" (code name: News), the private detective I hired to do a background check on Cabot, and dispatched him to uncover additional Tisdale tidbits. He found two.

Though the man represents himself as a Princeton graduate, regularly attending local Princeton Club functions, investigation reveals he's never earned a diploma, thereby branding himself a liar as well as a womanizing cheat.

Further, there's the matter of his brief employment at Charles Schwab, brief due to dismissal for unspecified improprieties. Might this character tutti frutti even include a criminal topping?

Isobel sat atop this information like a hen hatching a rare egg, awaiting the suitable moment to crack it over the head of her cherished friend.

10

DAISY HUMMEL and Reggie Burbage had been classmates at Ottumwa High in Iowa and, like most girls, she was smitten instantly by the boy's wavy brown hair, his long eyelashes, and a voice that conveyed the warmth of glowing embers.

True, he was somewhat self-centered, but he confessed to Broadway aspirations, and weren't all actors a bit fond of themselves? Daisy was not the prettiest girl in the class—her figure more sturdy than alluring—and she was prone to clumsiness. Yet, most important and most flattering, Reggie made it clear that of all his admirers he fancied *her*.

Together they made a daring decision; risking her father's fury, they eloped. They were on a train to New York City when Daisy's ear detected a transformation in her new husband. Since leaving Ottumwa, Reggie had acquired an English accent! He walked around with one hand cupped to an ear, critiquing resonance and vowel placement.

To placate her troubled parents Daisy promised she'd indulge Reggie's acting experiment for five years, and should nothing promising occur, they'd return home and accept real life.

But in the interim both parents perished in an auto accident, willing her a fortune accrued from meat packing, while Reggie became disenchanted with rejection. "Deuced difficult for talent to thrive, old dumpling," he told his wife, "when the theatre is run by incompetents and ignoramuses. I love the profession far too much to compromise myself."

So another train transported Mr. and Mrs. Burbage to the other coast, where they discovered Loma Bella, California. Once their membership application to Elsinore was approved, they bought a Tudor home Reggie christened Wilde House, on Gertrude Circle. But Daisy knew their happiness could never be complete without a platform for Reggie to demonstrate his talent. So she set off in search of a theater she ultimately found in downtown Loma Bella, a disused movie house called the Romero, that she altered into a state-of-the-art theater.

Reggie appointed himself artistic director, meaning he had liberty to choose the material, the role he wanted to play, and authority to direct his amateur cast. The Burbages plunged into the local swim with a big splash. Already established in the pool was Mary Clarke, as she was known then, who complemented Reggie's urbanity to perfection. Of course, her British accent was genuine. Audiences acclaimed the couple's chemistry as incandescent.

Always the centerpiece at cocktail parties, lounging in the sunshine of compliments, Reggie liked to say, "I believe I can play just about anything, but Shaw, Wilde, and Coward suit me right down to the ground. There's no writer like the Bard, of course, but I fear—" and here he gestured disarmingly—"these brain cells might disappoint me during the loveliest passages."

The local newspaper, the Loma Bella *Sun*, toadied shamelessly to all Romero productions because of income derived from Daisy's advertisements. Its drama critic was under orders to write reviews suitable for pasting in her scrapbook.

But the man skipped town in quest of his self-respect, abandoning the post to a woman from San Francisco who either hadn't been told the ground rules or perhaps deliberately ignored them. After watching Reggie perform a second time, this person, named Caitlin Wills, wrote, "Mr. Burbage is, as usual, in fine voice, and from a list I've seen of past Romero productions, it would appear the company is mired in a time warp somewhere between the Edwardian era and 1925. For the sake of his audiences, one wishes Mr. Burbage might accept more contemporary challenges, that he might stretch his instrument to sound fresher notes."

No living organism in Loma Bella was more thrilled to read this rebuke than Isobel von Braun, nauseated by bouquets showered on Cabot's pretentious Bohemians. All these years she'd had to swallow bile, recognizing any voiced negative opinion of Romero offerings was tactless; the theater was reckoned above reproach. She must bide her time. She needed a catastrophe to occur before she coiled and struck, and she got it.

Many actors profess they never read notices of their work; Daisy learned better. Reggie was infuriated by the critic's reprimand.

"Diminish my talent, will she?"

"Calmly, dear," Daisy said. "You could have a stroke."

"I'll show her!" Leaving breakfast untasted, he strode to the front door.

"Where are you going?"

He turned, timing a dramatic exit. "To the library!"

Reggie rummaged through one anthology after another of contemporary plays before inspiration seized him.

It was mid-afternoon when he made a dramatic reappearance. "I've got it, old hen," he cried triumphantly, brandishing his selection. "A classic Tennessee Williams play called *A Streetcar Named Desire*. The leading role is so juicy I can taste it."

Daisy knew a lot about money but nothing about the theater. "What role is that, dear?"

"A chap named Stanley Kowalski."

Isobel von Braun was among first-nighters who witnessed the disaster. The crisp Mayfair accent emerging from the mouth of a boorish cretin thoroughly confused Reggie's fans, and the sexual innuendoes made little sense because the star, conscious of physical shortcomings, refused to strip to an undershirt.

Von Braun scuttled backstage to eavesdrop on inevitable insincerities. Even loyalist Lady Louise was hard-pressed for positive remarks. "You were magnificent as always, Reggie dear. But I fear the material was beneath you. So sordid. Such a waste of superlative talent."

Next day Isobel bought twenty copies of the *Sun* to distribute to people who might have missed reading Caitlin Wills's judgment that last evening an atrocity had been committed on the stage of the Romero.

"Were you there?" Isobel crowed to anyone in earshot. "Did you see? Beyond description!"

"Appalling. Dreadful," Ashley Faye concurred.

"That asinine English accent!" Isobel continued. "Which, by the way, is totally false, completely assumed."

"What? It certainly sounds real," said a confounded Libby Clarke. "I mean, like yourselves I hear rumors. But are you sure? How do you know?"

Isobel inclined her head, a mother superior dispensing wisdom to novitiates. "Let's just say I know this for a *fact*."

The price was cheap, a five thousand dollar fee for News, plus three hundred a day per diem, to interview high school classmates of both Reggie and Daisy, who remembered both as having dialects as cornfed as their own.

Isobel was riding the crest of momentum. "But none of you darlings were seated where I was, in the very front row, to see the punishment being inflicted on Blanche DuBois. The man has such a fetish about enunciating his vowels, it creates saliva that must perforce be ejected. From my vantage, looking past the footlights, I witnessed the shower our poor Mary was made to endure."

Ashley had an intuition. "She may have been so sickened she'll never act again."

Libby had a conviction. "Had I been humiliated so, I would retire."

Isobel concluded, "The Romero Players are finished."

The Romero Players would never be finished, not so long as Daisy Burbage was writing the checks. In addition to inheriting riches sufficient to support an Elsinore lifestyle and Reggie's productions, she'd also inherited Walter Hummel's Iowa work ethic.

Daisy could not abide being idle. Long ago she'd accepted there'd never be a family of her own; Reg preferred being an only child. Nor were meaningless bridge parties and charity luncheons her idea of activity. She craved action.

She asked herself, what better arena than real estate? She earned a license in record time, then designated herself unofficial agent for all available Elsinore properties. Studying plans of the club's one hundred and fifty-two acres she calculated, at a half acre apiece, the grounds had space to accommodate two hundred additional homes. At a six percent agent fee this would finance Reggie's ambition to stage the complete works of Eugene O'Neill.

Since new members were required to pay an initiation fee of seventy thousand dollars, the club got rich, too. Yet expansion had stubborn opponents, especially among original members like von Braun and Cabot, who complained about the proximity of houses, increased traffic, more difficulty getting dinner reservations at the best tables, and a decline in admission standards.

Or as Selena put it, "These *nouveaux* are disgustingly tacky."

And Isobel asked, "Have you seen the eyesore being constructed in Horatio Hollow? Another coup for our shameless Ms. Burbage. She sold the property to a proctologist!"

Together they shivered. They would have cut Daisy, had there been opportunity, but their nemesis was too busy to attend social functions. Then they decided they'd get their point across by resigning from Daisy's book club, little realizing the group had been disbanded months before.

The sole remaining alternative was to boycott Reggie Burbage productions at the Romero, but given their joint participation in *Kiss Me Kate*, how in the world could they do that?

The shameless Ms. Burbage was bullet-proof.

From her garret at Versailles, Selena Cabot saw a dinner was about to take place across the fairway in Hydrangea and knew the guest list, thanks to enduring July light and Bausch and Lomb binoculars with their zoom function. She saw the toothy Ashley Faye and her drunken husband dismount from their yellow Lexus, followed minutes later by the womanizer Baxter Clarke and his stout new wife in their black BMW. Earlier she'd observed von Braun's chef, Wong, make two trips to remove four paper bags of groceries from his Chevy and guessed, correctly, he'd been ordered to shop for blander fare than that

served by her Jewel. It was certain to be the same old menu: to-
mato soup, roast beef cooked too rare, Yorkshire pudding, pop-
overs, salad with inedible walnut dressing, and fattening chocolate sundaes for dessert.

From her place at head of the table, Isobel approved her seating arrangement of the Sensible People—Kippy at the end opposite her, where he might charm the two ladies at either side,
this evening her *protegée* Ashley Faye and Baxter's new bride,
Libby.

At one time Ashley had been little more than a stranger, Isobel remembered, but that was before she accepted my invitation to attend a service at Saint Cecilia. Since then her energy
has infused the church, enriching it as in-house marriage counselor. To those who dare belittle this mission by pointing out
Ashley herself has been married five times, I cry, "That's the
point; she's so experienced! There's no person better qualified
to treat marital distress."

Of course, Libby Clarke is still something of a social novelty,
a round little thing with many chins and that prodigious bosom.
But she projects an innocence that puts the lie to rumors she's a
shoplifter. Why, a teeny percentage of her oil revenue could buy
every market in California!

Isobel had seated Baxter on her left, where she might bask in
his manly attentions. Dressed tonight in an impeccably tailored
suit—"It's Brooks Brothers," he admitted—it's a fact my dear
friend has become more fashion-conscious since marrying Libby.

On my right I placed Ashley's fifth husband, Trevor Faye. If I
were she, I might have made a happier choice, but after four
failures perhaps her options were exhausted. Certainly this time
she's married financial security. Trevor's forebears were extraor-
dinarily clairvoyant; they bought up Colorado mountain properties to build America's most popular ski resorts.

The skilled hostess addressed her table. "Gracious, aren't we fortunate this is a Sunday so we might have the company of our two artists, Libby and Baxter?" She turned to him. "Spies who've attended Romero rehearsals tell me you're stealing the show."

He shook his head in wonder. "I never thought I'd see the day when making a fool of myself was fun."

To include the inebriated Trevor, Isobel complimented him. "It's my understanding, sir, you are a champion golfer; champion, I believe, of Elsinore?" She saw why people wished he didn't drink so much, though some suggested it was anesthetic to his wife's unrelenting cheer.

"I s'pose. I play a lot."

"It must be marvelous exercise."

Using his napkin to stifle a belch, Trevor said, "Nothing like a gulp of fresh air."

Obligations fulfilled, Isobel elevated her voice. "Everyone, attention please—I have wonderful news! Our dear friend and neighbor Arthur Auchincloss tells me he and his new wife are ready at last to emerge from seclusion. In fact, only tonight my charming houseguest Rolf accepted their dinner invitation."

"Best invite them quickly, Snookums," Kip said, "before our friend across the fairway strikes first."

"Shame, Kippy. Lovely Selena opens her arms to everyone. The rumor she and I are involved in some sort of disagreement is totally false. Why, just yesterday we went birding together. It was refreshing to see the binoculars she trains on us being used for more seemly pursuits."

Ashley said, "You are a living saint, Isobel, to rise above such continued discourtesy."

"It's in the scriptures, isn't it, dear? It's no sacrifice, is it, to turn the other cheek? A pity Selena has yet to heed the beckoning of Our Savior."

Libby said, "What do you expect? She's surrounded by all those Bohemians, don't you see? When I was married to Judge Horace I can't tell you the number of times I had to bite my tongue to avoid saying something unwise."

Noticing guests had finished the entree, Isobel extended a foot under the table, searching for the hidden buzzer that sounded a kitchen summons. In so doing, her shoe was misdirected several inches to the left, where it pressed Baxter's ankle suggestively.

From his expression, she worried her intention had been misconstrued.

Before huddling with cast and crew, Reggie sent for his set designer, Morgan Ball. The enormous woman, a sculptress in private life, carried drawings she'd made to illustrate her presentation.

"This is what I have in mind, Reg," she said. "K.I.S.S. Keep it simple, stupid, right? Look around and you'll see half the battle's already won." He looked, uncomprehending. "I'm talking about the bare backstage itself, for God's sake. We have the one flight of stairs that leads to actual dressing rooms that'll serve the same purpose for us. So—all we need to do"—and here she unrolled a design to demonstrate—"is build a little room like this, supposedly the doorman's office. We put it downstage right, and outside we put in a pay phone, where the Gangsters call their capo and so forth."

"Lovely, dear," said Reggie. "Smashing."

"Wait. The other three sets I put on rollers. Look at this," and she unfurled another drawing. "Here you see the adjoining dressing rooms of Lilli and Fred, with a door between, the tables already set up with props. My brawny beauties join me in muscling the set onto marks already made on the floor in fluorescent paint."

"Ah. Clever," said Reg.

"Hold your water, we have two more. This guy," uncovering a mockup of a theater stage entrance, "for the 'Too Darn Hot' number—"

"Wonderful, wonderful."

"And then the third roll-on, this for the play-within-a-play. Look at this—Presto, change-o. Bam. Now we're in Padua."

"My gracious," Reg enthused, pressing the edges of the drawing to appreciate it more fully. "I'd swear we were in vintage Italy."

"Look here," Morgan continued, pointing. "This represents the door to Baptista's house, where Bianca and Kate enter and exit—see? And here—upstage left—is where I've put the window to Kate's room above."

"Good heavens. Remarkable."

Morgan punched his shoulder. "How 'bout that? Three sets on wheels."

Reggie shook his head in admiration. "Dear, dear."

"And last," said Morgan climactically, "because we need a drop curtain to conceal set changes, I thought I'd have a little fun, inject a little humor here. I mean, we're dealing with a star whose ego is bigger than a breadbox, right? Look at this."

It was a painting. Reggie read:

"The Taming of the Shrew"
A Musical
Entire Production Conceived, Delivered,
Directed by and also Starring
FREDRIC C. GRAHAM

Book by Wm. Shakespeare

"Haw haw," rhapsodized Reg, wincing from another punch on the shoulder.

11

REGINALD BURBAGE assembled his entire company on the Romero stage to tell them how he, impersonating an objective audience eye, visualized the production. All sat on camp chairs, holding scripts, pens at the ready.

"Now then," the director said, "to begin at the beginning. Cast, for simpler identification, I shall abstain from calling you by character names because most of you have two, counting the play-within-a-play. Instead I'll refer to you as Selena, Rolf, and so on. Understood?"

At their nods he continued, "During the first number, 'Another Op'nin', Another Show,' our choreographer Velvet has a stunning vision of moving you all about, seemingly at random. Each of the principals is introduced by arriving separately, coming downstage so we recognize their importance—first Kip, then Bunny, and finally Selena. She's dressed like a movie star—you have that, Lady Louise?—including strands of pearls, perhaps?"

"Pearls? You shall have them," the costumer said.

"Selena, a taxi has just taken you from your Baltimore hotel to deposit you at the stage door. These people milling about are all strangers to you. You're a bit apprehensive—you haven't appeared on a stage in some years, after all—yet you're stimulated by the challenge, drawn as if by magnet to the footlights, where you stare first at the orchestra, then up to the balcony. You're remembering when you last performed, remembering it was in a play with Rolf, remembering how happy your marriage had been.

"Seymour, old chap, when she takes that position, squarely downstage center, dim the stage lights and isolate her with a pin spot. You follow?"

Lighting director Katz pushed his glasses higher on his nose. "You want full figure? Head and shoulders?"

"Full figure." As Seymour wrote Reggie went on, "Libby, darling, this is your cue. You segue from 'Another Op'nin' to 'So In Love.' I want you to bring the fullest emotion to playing the song, dear; your craving for Baxter, perhaps? As Selena listens, the lyrics as yet unvoiced, we see the passion that once existed between her and Rolf. At the song's conclusion, Selena, the spell is broken. You drop your head and seat yourself on an upstage chair, a cue to you, Seymour, to restore the prior lighting, and to you, Libby, to return to playing the opening number.

"At its conclusion, enter Rolf, brisk and full of himself, anxious to stage the curtain calls. The dialogue informs us of Selena's suspicion Rolf is having an affair with Bunny. Next we're introduced to the pair's abiding animosity when Rolf says, 'Isn't a smile in your contract, Miss Vanessi?' and she calls you 'Bastard!'

"Remember, loves, it's the first anniversary of your divorce. You both wish it had never happened, but it did, because of your ego, Rolf, and because of your temper, Selena. It's impossible for you to overplay those qualities; you have my full permission to play ego and temper to the hilt.

"This," said Reggie, "brings us to our second relationship, an unhappy one, actually. Early in Act One we learn that Bunny is in love with Kip, who appears to be simply using her. He returns from a night of gambling during which he's lost ten thousand dollars. Because his credit's no longer good, he signs Rolf's name to an IOU, having little regret for the deception because Rolf's been pursuing his girlfriend...A side note here, Lady Louise; when Bunny's in rehearsal costume we want to show as much flesh as the law allows."

"Mrs. von Braun may not be pleased to see that."

"Not to fear. I shall explain to our patroness. After all, Arthur's given his consent."

Auchincloss shrugged and sniffed. "No big deal. It's only skin."

"In any event," Reggie continued, "Bunny's a sad little thing, uneducated, with just one goal in life, to be a Broadway star, and she'll do whatever's necessary to make that happen. She and Kip have been a dance team in clubs, and this is the closest she's come to the prize. Kip's gambling threatens to ruin everything, as she expresses in the sweetly chiding ballad, 'Why Can't You Behave?'"

"An acting note here, Kippy. You're the cock of the walk, as it were, and I want everything about you to say that. Your walk is a strut, you wear your fedora at an angle over your eyes, you react to women like a rooster in a hen house."

Kip sighed. "I'll give it my best, Reg."

"Remember, Bunny is your *slave*. You are the world's greatest lover."

The actor used a pen to scratch his head. "You don't think that people might find this—well, a bit thick? After all, Bunny's taller than I am."

"Kippy, *believe*."

Morgan Ball spoke up. "Let me get this straight. At the end of 'Another Op'nin' the lights come down?" She looked to Seymour who was consulting his script.

"Correct."

"Okay," said Morgan. "The grips and I push like hell to roll the dressing room set onto the fluorescent paint marks."

Reggie added, "Yes. Selena and Rolf will already be seated inside. The lights will come up only after you and your roustabouts are offstage, once the dialogue begins with Rolf complaining about poor attendance. 'Well, so much for a Hollywood name,' he says. 'Your fans must have heard you were appearing in person.'"

"Next we have the telephone call from Selena's White House

fiancé." He raised his voice to shout, "You have that marked in your script, do you, Judge Horace? The cue for making the phone ring?"

The sound technician was smiling attentively, not having heard. Wife Mary tapped his arm, pointing to the red mark in the margin of his script. "The phone cue, darling. Here."

"Yes, yes," he said. "Of course. The phone." He pressed the button on a battery-powered device, causing a ringing sound.

"Jolly good," the director said.

Indicating a biscuit tin alongside, the Judge asked, "You want to hear the crash box, too?"

"Not at the moment, thank you."

Tallmadge pointed to a wheel. "You want me to crank up the siren?"

"Later, Judge," Reggie said. "Anyway, we go on with the sparring. After Selena flaunts her large engagement ring, Rolf says, 'Is that the Hope Diamond, the one with the curse?', and off we go into reminiscences of their lives together. She's saved the cork from a bottle of champagne consumed at their wedding breakfast, we learn they both worked, Selena reading tea leaves, Rolf demonstrating shaving soap at Woolworth's, and so on until Libby gives us a lead-in to the silly operetta they performed together, *The Prince of Potsdam*, which takes us to—"

Rolf said, "'Wunderbar'."

"Yes," said Reggie, "and a marvelous opportunity for shameless hamming. Both of you—carry on joyously, romping about, holding hands, climbing up on the couch, waltzing until you collapse with laughter. For it's in that breathless moment you recall something more serious, how very much you loved each other. No words necessary. The look does it. You join in a passionate kiss. Even the untoward entrance of the stage manager cannot break the spell, causing Selena to ask wistfully, 'Whose fault was it?' Naturally Rolf says, 'It could have been your temper.' And

Selena replies, 'It could have been your ego.' And there we leave it for the nonce, an ember, so to speak, awaiting the prod of a fire tong.

"Moving on, we come to the comic element of the piece, in the personae of our two Gangsters, come to collect an IOU Rolf did not write. It's typical our star isn't intimidated in the least, assuming incorrectly these are two fans who've come to beg his autograph. The man's vanity is sublime.

"Now, Baxter and Hugh, you are, of course, a pair of thugs, but let's make some differentiation here. Baxter—you being the larger man, let's assume you're the one who uses muscle to scare people, while Hugh typically brandishes a gun. Further, Hughie, I'd like you to glue on a mustache and carry an omnipresent cigar. Another point, gentlemen: When you address Rolf it's always as 'Mr. Gray-Ham,' an unappreciated slight. The Spewaks have given you some of the best lines in the play, so don't be afraid to milk them, like the reference to Rolf's lapse of memory. 'The man has magnesia.' 'Yeah, we cure it.'

"So our hoodlums leave temporarily, promising to return, while the plot thickens with the delivery of flowers to Selena, who's amazed and touched. She says, 'Snowdrops, pansies and rosemary—my wedding bouquet. He didn't forget,' which cues the vocalizing of 'So In Love.' "

Reggie called to his wife, "Daisy darling, I've no notion what these particular flowers actually look like, but some members of the audience may, so let's be accurate, shall we? Make the imitations as real as possible?"

Daisy was shaking her pen. "I've run out of ink. But I'll remember."

"Darling, I'd feel more confident if you made a note. Would someone be kind enough to lend my wife a writing instrument?... Thank you, Arthur.

"I shall be choosing specific moments during the singing, Selena, when I want you to reach out to Rolf, as it were, by placing your hands on the closed door to his dressing room, and Rolf, I shall be informing you of those selfsame moments, because nostalgia will cause you to mirror what she does, in a desire to touch her again. At the conclusion of the number, Selena, I'd like you to slump down with your back against the door, and from the opposite side Rolf's back will be pressed against yours."

The director sat straight and clapped his hands. "Right, then! We're close to *The Taming of the Shrew,* the play-within-a-play. We begin with Rolf putting on his tunic, admonishing his dresser for having admitted two Mafia people, which leads to the awful revelation his flowers, intended for Bunny, were delivered instead to Selena. Hoping it's not too late, he sneaks into her dressing room and is in the act of filching the bouquet when she appears and reclaims it. Rolf lunges for the note. Too late. She snatches it away, forcing him into fast talking, inventing a lie about the note's content. Flattered, she asks, 'Do you really mean that?' 'With all my heart,' he replies. 'Then that's where the card is going, next to mine,' she says, and stuffs it down her bosom.

"As a footnote here, Selena darling, remember there's a subtext. Tonight is the opening of your first theatrical venture in many years, and you'd be suffering a severe case of nerves.

"Cue music to 'A Troupe of Strolling Players Are We,' leading to 'We Open in Venice,' all four of our principals performing a charming dance in front of the drop curtain. When it rises we're outside Lord Peter's home in Padua. Now we hear actual words penned by the Bard, who tells us Bunny cannot marry until Selena's been married first. We also see and hear why she's a tough sell, as it were, appearing at her upstairs window to vilify any man in sight, beginning with her poor father, Lord Peter. One after the other, she flings three flower pots at the man.

"A note here to my props person: Daisy darling, we know

Lord Peter is athletic, but to catch three objects without dropping any, let's be sure the pots are lightweight? Balsa, perhaps,
or something of the sort?" He looked to be sure his wife was
writing. She was.

"Our fiery-tempered shrew hasn't finished. From the window
she hurls out a three-legged stool. It's unnecessary, gentlemen,
to make more than an attempt to catch it. If one of you can,
fine, but don't put yourselves in jeopardy.

"Once Selena slams the window shut, we're left with Bunny,
Kip, and our two new friends, Tad and Chauncey. They woo the
young lady with the 'Marry Me' introduction to what will become 'Tom, Dick or Harry.'" Reg cleared his throat to rid it of
awkward impediment. "First off, Bunny, I should tell you our
Mr. Porter is being exceedingly naughty here. By that I mean—
he emphasizes one of the three names as representing—"

"She's ahead of you, Burbage," Auchincloss grumbled. "She
wasn't born yesterday."

"Of course not. But dear me, Velvet, I worry about the stam-
ina required of the trio to complete the dance number as you've
choreographed it. I approve of you featuring Tad rather than
Kip, because Tad has some background as an acrobat, but I fear
all three will be so winded at the close we won't understand the
lyrics."

The choreographer's exasperation was unconcealed. "But
it's...you can't—oh, hell. Okay. I'll tone it down a little."

Glancing again at his notes, Reggie continued, "My compliments to you, Lady Louise. I've seen the costumes and they're
simply smashing."

She beamed. "I hoped you'd like them. I rented them all
from Free Your Fantasy at a reasonable price."

"Good show." The director again referred to his notes. "Now
then, plunging on, we next have Rolf's entrance, singing the
boastful 'I've Come to Wive It Wealthily in Padua.' Kip warns

the braggart he's in over his head, a statement authenticated by a scream and crash from offstage.... Allow me to interrupt my-elf—Mary, are you certain Judge Horace is familiar with the crash box?"

"Oh, yes."

"Then may I inquire what's inside that metal biscuit tin, be-sides glass, of course?"

"There's also a cup, a few wooden blocks, marbles, and coins. When it's shaken it creates a wonderful racket."

Reggie smiled uncertainly. "I can imagine, dear, if only we hear it on cue." He turned to assistant stage manager Buster Rooney, an ingenuous, freckle-faced student at Loma Bella High. "Buster, you indispensable boy, you have this particular cue underlined in red ink?"

"I have it underlined for sure, Mr. Burbage."

The octogenarian was smiling idiotically, hoping to please, confused by the frowns trained on him. Mary patted his arm.

Reggie shook his head and sighed. "So! Despite the warn-ings, our overconfident swain wagers that he will conquer 'Katherine the Cursed.' At this point there's a scream and Bun-ny exits the house pursued by Selena swinging a broom intend-ed to decapitate. She chases her younger sister back into the house, and when Kip and others try to intervene they're chased into the house as well.

"This clears the stage to leave our shrew all alone, prepared to share her feelings in singing 'I Hate Men.' Once again, magi-cal Selena, it's Katie-bar-the-door, if you'll forgive the pun. The woman's outrageous behavior is what the play is all about, don't you know, so do your worst—shriek, snarl, bark like a dog, what-ever extravagance comes to mind. And on the final shout of the lyrics, prove your hatred by clearing the table where the men have just had a meal—send all the plates and cups flying in a clatter. It's all tin, is it not, darling Daisy?"

"Worthless. Cheapest items on my budget."

Selena asked, "Aren't you worried about the mess?"

"Before the next scene begins Morgan and her brawny crew will have cleared the wreckage. Am I right, dear?"

The set designer's pen was at work. "You got it, big guy."

"So our virago sashays toward the house, but before reaching the door she steps out of character, removes a note from her bodice, waves it at Petruchio, kisses it and teases, 'Fred'—?"

"Uh oh," said Rolf.

"Exactly. Reckoning is in the air. As you and Lord Peter begin your dialogue, Judge Horace hopefully gives us another volley from his crash box, and from offstage we hear Selena shout 'Bastard!' As the dowry bartering begins we see Selena open her upstairs window, no longer play-acting, now genuinely infuriated."

"Beneath her, standing in his accustomed macho posture, Rolf sings 'Were Thine That Special Face.' Please note, Libby, this should be played to a bolero beat."

The pianist held up the sheet music. "I have it marked," she said.

"At the close, enter Selena holding a bouquet Rolf has sent her, saying, 'Were Thine That Special Face—hah!' and hurls the flowers at him. In the Bard's words she says 'Speak, Petruchio. So thy message is not meant for me—you bastard!'

"The epithet, of course, is not in the text, and although the ensuing physical combat is suggested, it's carried out with a gusto that would have startled Shakespeare. She punches Rolf in the stomach, she strangles him, slaps him, bites him, kicks him—"

Selena interrupted. "Wait, wait, Reggie. Hold it. Please stop. I've been wanting to talk to you about this for ages." Her frustration was expressed by twisting in her chair. "What worries me is the amount of violence Rolf and I are asked to pretend. I realize it's all to goad him into the retaliation that ends the scene, where he stretches me across the table and spanks me, but—"

"Darling, we need all of it," Reggie said earnestly, "and not simply to vindicate his response. We need it to cover clenched-teeth asides like, 'You keep acting like this, Miss Vanessi, I'll give you the paddling of your life,' 'I'm warning you,' and after your final slap, 'Now you're going to get it.'"

"But how can I do all the punching, kicking, and slapping without harming Rolf the actor, who's a very nice man?"

"Selena, don't worry," said the victim. "There's nothing less believable than pulled punches; be as rough as you please."

"But I *don't* please. Acting is all about pretending."

"Lovely lady, I can't *pretend* to paddle your bottom."

"But that's different; I'll wear padding. You can be as extreme as you want." Sensing she'd become tiresome, Selena closed the subject with a joke. "Okay, objection overruled; I rather enjoy pain."

Reggie chuckled, then continued, "Well, then, following the spanking we drop the curtain and hear all hell break loose, another opportunity for Judge Horace and his crash box. We see Mary, as stage manager Ralph, sprint out to pick up props left behind. The curtain rises on the backstage set, Selena and Rolf still caterwauling enroute to their dressing rooms. She calls Bunny 'that Copa canary.' He says, 'I couldn't teach you manners as a wife, but by God I'll teach you manners as an actress.' Of course, she slaps him before slamming her door.

"In continuing rage Selena phones her fiancé the General to complain of abuse and tells him she's quitting immediately. Rolf threatens to have her brought up on charges at Equity. On return to his dressing room, who should appear? Tweedle Dum and Tweedle Dee, our two Gangsters, demanding settlement. A light bulb goes on for Rolf. He shrugs and tells them, 'I'd have it by the end of the week, but—.' Well, naturally the hoodlums take charge, demanding that Selena finish out the week.

"Following the offstage wedding of Petruchio and Kate, Rolf appears, literally cracking a whip to subdue his new bride. To intensify Selena's ignominy, she now has two babysitters, Baxter and Hugh." He looked to Lady Louise. "I adore the costumes you chose for the boys. They're superbly ludicrous—Hugh with the absurd mustache and Baxter with the blond wig."

"I feel like an ass," Baxter complained.

"That's how you *should* feel," Reggie told him. "*Both* of you. How often do hoodlums set foot on a stage, eh? Hughie, when you first realize you're standing in front of a large audience I want you to convey your terror with moaning sounds. You feel in such jeopardy, you reach for a gun that Baxter orders you to put away.

"The act's closing number, the singing of 'Kiss Me Kate' should be desperate farce, Rolf singing 'Kiss Me,' Selena resisting with furious arpeggios of 'No!,' until at last she uses her favorite word, calling him 'Bastard!,' forcing Rolf to improvise by singing 'Oh, Katie, that's a naughty word. Kiss me,' puckering his lips hopefully as she trills variations on 'Bastard.' Meantime, our mobsters circle around, uncertain of their roles, except when Selena threatens physical harm, when they interpose themselves in protection of Rolf.

"At last, standing behind her, sick of the interminable nonsense, Baxter says, 'Aw, kiss him' and he thrusts her away."

"Selena," said Rolf. "Just let the momentum of the shove carry you to me. I'll lower my shoulder, like this, so you're able to collapse over it, and then I'll bear you off in a fireman's carry."

"Bravo," said Reggie. "End of Act One…Daisy, pet, skipping ahead to props required after intermission, please remember when Arthur enters as General Harrison Howell, he'll be escorted by two soldiers bearing rifles. Have you procured the rifles?"

His wife riffled through her notebook. "I don't see anything about rifles."

"We need rifles, my love; we must get them…Do you see anything about a corncob pipe?"

After continued riffling, "Yes, here it is. Corncob pipe."

"It shouldn't be just any old corncob pipe, dear; it should be an outsized corncob pipe. He's emulating General Douglas MacArthur, don't you see."

Daisy's shoulders slumped, evidently crushed beneath the weight of responsibility. "I have no idea where I'll find such a thing, but—couldn't we do without it?"

There was edginess in Reggie's voice. "We could do without any number of things, dear, but then we wouldn't have much of a show, would we? Perhaps I should have a word with our producer."

"That might be a good idea."

"Daisy darling, *you're* the producer." She placed her face in her hands. Worried he'd gone too far, Reggie changed the subject. "Arthur, old chap, yours is an absolute pip of a part. The character is so arrogant, so Hitlerian, so much what you Americans call a 'stuffed shirt.'" He paused, observing the actor. "It's—well, it's going to take all of your acting skills to bring it off."

"I can handle it, Burbage."

"And do give us that sniff you do. It's bloody marvelous."

"What sniff?"

Reg felt the flesh at his waist being pinched. He turned to meet Bunny's expressionless gaze. "I mean—never mind." He coughed. "Take ten, everyone."

During the intermission Selena sat in place at the table, wearing a smirk, her mind miles distant from Padua and just as far from the Romero. She was revisiting the moment when her binoculars lingered on the rose garden across the fairway, noticing the rare Belle of Portugal and Joseph's Coat were thriving—to no purpose. She was cognizant von Braun's sole remaining social ambition was membership in the Loma Bella Garden Club, a reward to be withheld forever, thanks to a quiet conversation with Lady Louise.

I simply don't understand it, Isobel lamented. My garden at Hydrangea is glorious, scrupulously maintained by a corps of Mexicans, yet my petition for membership in the Garden Club is consistently ignored. In heaven's name, why? This so frustrated me, at last I abased myself to beg member Mary Tallmadge to confess the reason.

I was being blackballed by the club president, Lady Louise Glenn!

"But why?" I wailed.

Discomfited, Mary stammered out some story of how I was being punished for having spread a damaging rumor about Lady Glenn's close friend, Reggie Burbage.

"What sort of rumor?"

After hesitation, Mary spelled it out. "You tell people Reggie is a cross-dresser."

I suppressed the urge to cry out, Well, he is! You should have seen for yourself, as I did. I was strolling innocently along the sixth fairway when I passed the bedroom window at Wilde House, and there was Reggie, laying Daisy's nightgowns out on their bed. Intrigued, naturally, I paused to observe from behind a clump of bushes, watching as, one by one, he took them to a mirror and held them in front of him by the straps. Could there be more damning evidence?

Instead I scoffed, "Cross-dresser! You and I both know such an accusation is rubbish; I never said any such thing. What I *may* have said, probably to a person hard of hearing, was, 'Reggie appears cross for such a fancy dresser.' Oh how horrid, to be castigated so unjustly. Promise me, Mary, you will carry the truth to Lady Louise!'"

After a year elapsed, a period of useless expectation, I conceded I had been judged persona non grata.

Vengeance! I cried. Anything to repay the spiteful woman!

So I dispatched my private investigator to Vancouver, at a fee of five thousand dollars plus three hundred a day per diem, to get the goods on the Glenns. The man returned with disappointing news. Peter had purchased the title of Lord from an impoverished Canadian royalist, and therefore it was his to use as he pleased.

Lying in my own blood on the marble of the Forum, I prayed for a chance to retaliate, a prayer answered from an unexpected source. My assassins, mistakenly believing I was dead, were taken unawares when I brandished a fatal knife handed me by Monica, manager at the Wee Willow Club.

"Mrs. von Braun, I am in receipt of an application for membership submitted by a Mrs. Selena Cabot. As chairperson of the admissions committee, would you endorse the application?"

I was astounded my enemy would expose herself so carelessly. The Wee Willow Club, after all, was merely a downtown luncheon rendezvous for women who'd wearied themselves during a morning's shopping. It was prestigious in its own way, of course, but nothing like the Garden Club. Did Cabot sincerely believe a person so unjustly slandered would turn the other cheek?

I was torn. Should I heed the Christian generosity so esteemed at Saint Cecilia, or a tiny devil who'd somehow survived the cleansing of countless communions?

The imp won.

I said, "Monica dear, Mrs. Cabot is a valued friend who fits in well here at Elsinore. But I don't feel comfortable endorsing her for membership because—I tell you this candidly and in confidence—her implications about my fiancé have been too hurtful.

"Not to worry. She has a servant who can fix her lunch."

12

FEW ARGUED the most unenviable staff position at Elsinore was that of Club Manager, a turnstile that revolved victims in and out a door situated next to the mail desk. Puzzled pretenders were never told what crime had been committed to merit the sudden excommunication, because members, after all, were forever dissatisifed—with being seated at a poor table, or with the menu, or with changes to a room's decor. Their complaint was unending.

The Manager's desk had been cleaned out eleven times before stability arrived in the person of Otto Steiner, a graduate in Hotel Management at San Diego State. Though balding, Otto was vain, his salary spent on Nordstrom's most expensive suits. Though in truth a third-generation Californian, he pretended he'd recently got off the plane from Dusseldorf, because he'd noticed wealthy women dining in restaurants were drawn to European rhythms like moths to a flame. His subtle, rehearsed accent blended well with the posture of a Prussian officer, and his manner of bobbing his head in acquiescence to a request was a perfect blend of dignity and servility. Another weapon was unexpected, swift hand-kissing that sent ladies into convulsions of delight.

Exhaustive study of the membership set Otto's priorities. Without question the two most influential women were club pioneers Selena Cabot and Isobel von Braun. Contact lenses weren't required to recognize the two detested each other and would each insist on being seated at Table One.

Fortunately they rarely dined on the same evening, but if they did, Otto shrugged apology that one had made an earlier reservation and immediately seated the other at the farthest remove.

And now, he thought wryly, the two are presumed teammates, von Braun funding the production of *Kiss Me Kate*, while Cabot is the vehicle's star. Well, I can be sure the dining room will be jammed for at least a month, the length of the run, and I can be sure the air will be crackling with vindictive electricity. The ladies of Elsinore do have a habit of choosing sides.

On occasion rude people inquire why I've never married and of course I cannot give them an honest answer. I've learned all I want to know about wedded bliss from observing our membership; with few exceptions the females are selfish, demanding, and troublesome.

Do you think I'd willingly share the social life of their husbands, who huddle together like a kennel of whipped puppies? Well, Steiner, you've no right to consider yourself superior, because every time you're tempted to quit, all it takes to reconsider is your mirrored image in an Armani suit.

But God, the problems! The dueling charities! It's just my luck Loma Bella has more charities than New Zealand has sheep, and every woman in the club puts a fence around one to claim it as hers. Selena Cabot owns the Boys and Girls Club, just as Mrs. von Braun owns the Loma Bella Museum of Art. The philanthropy's good for club revenue, of course, a convenient excuse for luncheons with committees, supposedly to map strategy, when usually the time's spent washing down gossip with glasses of Chardonnay.

But I praise God for one mercy—the book clubs are out of

my jurisdiction because the meetings take place in private homes. To my relief! I've heard, for example, that one club is headed by Ashley Faye, by virtue of having once been introduced to Jackie Collins at a cocktail party. Her second qualification is willingness to purchase the novel under discussion, then pass it along. Her generosity has sponsored "the contemporaries," authors Collins, Barbara Taylor Bradford, Danielle Steel, and Judith Krantz.

Of course, a rival club sneers at this. Daisy Burbage deems such writing "modern trash." "Our club," she tells members proudly, "will read only the classics." I'm told that in the past year they've read *Forever Amber*, *Love Story*, *Bridges of Madison County*, and *Jonathan Livingston Seagull*. As club president it's Daisy's duty to buy copies, there being a waiting list at the public library.

Consequently, the abiding crisis between the dueling dowagers has so agitated the dueling book clubs no one seems clear whether one's allegiance should be to contemporary or classics, nor is it clear who's to be paying. I'm told it's become so worrisome neither club's reconvened, and a few ladies have given up reading altogether.

However, Steiner, the charity events *are* in your jurisdiction—Saturday night balls or dinner auctions where every week the same people gather, women clad in new, expensive dresses, appraising one another behind hooded eyes. It's something to see. As they chatter enthusiastically their minds are elsewhere, trying to recall if during their latest conversation one had mentioned an impending trip to Portugal.

The saving grace in all these affairs is Lord Peter Glenn. As emcee no one can touch him because, for starters, he has that trial lawyer voice that makes amplification unnecessary, and his fund of stories is seemingly endless.

When I complimented him he told me, "It's a simple trick; I

own Milton Berle's encyclopedia of jokes. I search by category to match the theme of the evening's event, eliminate all the blue material, then make choices."

And no man can match Lord Peter as auctioneer. His courtroom hectoring so embarrasses misers they worry that, if they don't pony up, they'll be jailed.

Well, the auctions are merely vexing; what I dread most are the balls. Why is it old people insist on behaving as though they were thirty years younger, outdoing one another in a show of vitality? These affairs are so perilous, my programmed line to 911 routinely summons as many as three ambulances in one evening. I tell you, it's a headache. I must be at hand to supervise members being carted off, then hurry back to tend to survivors.

Otto Steiner saw himself as the consummate puppeteer, at work behind the scenes, playing all the roles, pulling the strings, sending signals to his staff with a subtle nod or urgent gesture, all to ensure members and guests were accommodated in every particular.

His efficiency received few compliments (after all, wasn't his salary remuneration enough?), but he might have been pleased to hear a tribute muttered by Trevor Faye, who asked Baxter Clarke, "How in hell do you suppose the krauts ever lost the war?"

One cause of Otto's anxiety was currently out of his jurisdiction, for Selena Cabot was circumnavigating the golf course with her dearest friend.

"What's your impression of your leading man?" Lady Louise Glenn asked, breathless as always.

"So far, so good; he's handsome and he can sing. Other than that, I know little about him."

We'd commenced our weekday power walk, exactly two and three quarter miles as measured by a pedometer. I thought, what better way to keep in shape for *Kate's* rigorous songs and dances?

Louise and I make such a contrasting pair, observers might laugh. Hello out there, Nosy Parker, I'm the long-strider in a jogging ensemble from Robinson's, my friend Louise the much shorter woman in a lumpy sweat suit and golf cap, the one bustling like a hyperactive hen. Beyond simple exercise we find this fun. There being a rule servants are never to be seen outside the home, the paths are seldom occupied, so it's opportunity for chitchat.

Out of the blue, or rather the fog of this overcast morning, puffing Louise asked an unsettling question. "Dear, are you still planning to propose Hugh for club membership?"

I glanced to confirm the inquiry was well-intentioned. "Well—I really hadn't given it much thought, dear, though I know he enjoys golf, most especially his rounds with Lord Peter. I have a feeling he's still too busy to make the social commitment."

"But he's so well-educated! Imagine, a Princeton graduate!" I nodded and was conjuring a diversion when Louise went on, "I never finished at McGill University, you know."

"Never be ashamed!" I blurted. "I never attended college either, but I'm worth two dozen Wellesley von Brauns." Upset I'd allowed myself to become upset, I sought to explain. "I, too, tried to remedy insufficient schooling by taking classes in Adult Education. I needed something to do, you know, something to occupy my hours after losing Carter."

Louise looked up, astonished. "You attended classes here? In Loma Bella?"

"Yes." Should I proceed? Louise is, after all, a trusted intimate. "In fact, to share a small confidence I know you will never, ever mention to a single soul, Adult Ed was where I met my second husband."

Louise groaned under the weight of this information. "He was a student, too?"

"No, no, dear. Our class visited his studio downtown. I realize people rarely saw him at Elsinore because he was so dedicated to his work. I may have told you he was a sculptor, though not the conventional sort like our quaint Morgan Ball. No, Laszlo used a welding mask and blowtorch to shape metal figures." The recollection made me laugh. "Naturally, I couldn't invite friends to visit because you've never *seen* such a mess, the floor littered everywhere with bits and pieces."

"I'm hurt you never introduced me," Louise huffed. "It was as if you were concealing him for some reason or other. What was he like?"

"Well, he was foreign—Hungarian, actually, and incredibly handsome." The increased heartbeat of exercise so altered past to present that I foolishly went on. "He was also younger than I, candidly, and—well, let's just say it was difficult keeping up with him, and leave it at that."

Too late. Louise stopped, grabbed my hand and pulled me to a bench on the fourteenth tee. Wheezing, she said, "I am not proceeding a step further until you tell me all."

Should I? I've been carrying the guilt so long it might be healthy to dump some of it. So I took a deep breath and gazed afar to avoid Louise's eyes. "You know, it's always flattering when a woman is desired, as I'm sure you know in your relationship with Lord Peter, but Laszlo—well, I don't how to put this delicately, except to say the man was—well, he was—insatiable."

Louise was gasping. "Well, I've never—I mean, I'm not sure I under—you mean he—"

I'd gone too far to stop now. "Yes! I mean anytime, any place, in showers, on toilet seats, during parties and picnics, in autos and airplanes, you name it. It was exhausting!"

Louise's eyes were saucers, her mouth a capitalized "O". "Ohhhh," she finally exhaled. "You poor thing! How you must have suffered!"

I pressed a finger to her lips. "Not a word, dear heart."

My trusted friend could only nod. "I'm so—breathtaken, I—I need to walk the rest of the way."

"And I as well. The memories have caused my legs to cramp."

Of course, the conclusion to the story is something I can never share with a living soul, not Louise, not anyone, the memory of Laszlo's last night on this earth. The scalawag was such a tease! He incessantly paid homage to what he impishly nicknamed my "snapping turtle," on this occasion availing himself of its pleasure whilst mounted from behind.

Oh, my God! I called across the boundary of mortality. What on earth happened, what were you thinking, my darling? Were you leading some sort of Magyar cavalry charge when you suddenly gave a great shout, lurched to the side, then pitched to the floor?

Ah, my God!

Seeing my tears, Louise squeezed a hand in sympathy.

Isobel von Braun lowered her binoculars, perplexed. The poisonous pair, Cabot and Lady Louise, were overdue at Versailles, and investigation revealed why. They were walking slowly.

Had age overtaken them at last, putting a stop to this pitiful fitness charade? No, neither appeared to be limping. In fact, they were holding hands! Do you suppose—?

No. Unthinkable.

However, they *were* Bohemians, and there *was* that gigantic freak Morgan Ball, who had facial hair and the voice of a drill sergeant.

At Saint Cecilia many consider me the most devout person in the congregation—tither, teacher of children's Bible school, organizer of bake sales and pot luck dinners, an altogether committed, compassionate woman.

However, I must admit, though only to myself, I harbor the

teensiest amount of malice toward the duo who just disappeared inside Versailles. Selena inflicted the first wound when she slandered my innocent friend Baxter, and later Lady Louise, like a latterday Brutus, drove a second dagger into my heart.

The memory of that teachery transformed Isobel's expression into a mask of woe. It's essential I conjure a thought to reclaim my accustomed pleasantness and, searching, I succeeded, finding it in the lingering image of my enemies walking hand in hand.

Picking up the telephone I pressed the numbers of the private detective I'd once hired to do background checks on Cabot and the Glenns. Cabot's sole blemish, disappointingly, turned out to be those years squandered on the stage. Of course, there were those two husbands following the demise of the old man, both of whom died under mysterious circumstances, but nothing scandalous was to be proved.

Perhaps until now.

And while I'm digging, she thought, just where do you suppose Arthur Auchincloss unearthed his sluttish wife?

Before she became a musical celebrity, the ladies of Elsinore considered Bunny Auchincloss a thornier problem than pruning their roses. Even during peak playing hours the girl wandered the fairways barefoot, in cutoff shorts and shirt tied beneath her braless bosom, causing handicaps to soar. A remonstration from the Board, citing Section 3, Article 8 on Rules for Appropriate Attire, was rebuffed by her husband.

"That applies only to people who golf. Bunny doesn't play," he said.

"What am I to do?" Isobel asked Selena. "Arthur has given me splendid financial advice in the past. I mean, it's all well and good for him to risk his life consummating such dangerous wedlock, but I can't simply drop him for having raging hormones."

"I agree," said Selena. "We must at least attempt social contact. If the girl doesn't golf, perhaps she plays bridge?"

Isobel called Arthur to ask, and he said, "No."

"I see. Unhappily, I'm a bit old for tennis, but perhaps I can arrange—"

"She doesn't play tennis."

"A pity. Well, I'd invite her here to Hydrangea for a swim, but I know you have that enormous pool of your own."

Arthur sniffed. "Glad you brought that up, Isobel. Not everybody has a pool, you know. Bunny and I've been thinking it might be fun to throw a barbeque for all our buddies and let 'em throw each other in the deep end. You free Sunday?"

Isobel quickly replied, "You're sweet to ask, dear. Unhappily, I never learned to swim."

Grateful, too, for the invitation was Selena, who mourned the fact she was allergic to chlorine.

Lady Louise had a sudden visitation of influenza.

Mary Tallmadge had a technical rehearsal for *Kiss Me Kate*.

Ashley Faye deplored the coincidence of a church retreat.

Libby Clarke would be visiting friends in Beverly Hills.

Daisy Burbage was giving a charity luncheon for the Romero Players.

In sum, all the members of the fair sex were otherwise occupied.

So Arthur hosted a hugely successful stag party, serving beers and Bloody Marys to men avid to splash water on his wife. On advice of his physician, Judge Tallmadge did not attend, but Seymour Katz did, exposing skin paler than the underbelly of a flounder.

Arthur anticipated his guests would participate in courting rituals. He guessed Baxter Clarke would wear his briefest Speedo to preen and pose in front of Bunny, only to be miffed by her disinterest.

Lord Peter was more subtle. Obviously a leg man, he brought along a snorkel for clear underwater viewing.

Trevor Faye and Reggie Burbage lacked physiques for swimwear, so stationed themselves poolside for ambling angles of stimulation.

Hugh Tisdale, an unapologetic breast man, waded in with his Nikon clicking one waist exposure after another, then got out to train his lens down the girl's cleavage.

As Arthur expected, his wife ignored them all. With the exception, that is, of a newly discovered soul mate, Kip Perkins. The pair shrieked delight to learn their shared addiction to afternoon soap operas.

That's all it took. Once Bunny had charmed Isobel von Braun's fiancé, the case was closed, club social acceptance absolute.

To Arthur's relief.

Having been importuned a third time by Arthur Auchincloss to observe guests in his pool, ("No swimming required"), Selena told herself it would be impolite to refuse this invitation. Well, I'll drag my feet, she thought, and make a fashionably late appearance. Reviewing options in bedroom drawers and closets, she chose a wide sun hat, chic sunglasses and, under a white kaftan, a one-piece swimsuit with a colorful floral design. Should I drive? she wondered. No. Her high heels skirted the edge of fairways to the backyard gate of Bulls and Bears.

Sounds of squealing and sloshing announced the party was in progress. Admitting herself, she glanced at the water and saw costar Rolf cavorting with Judge Horace's granddaughters, Melanie and Melody, hefting each in turn into the air. Also immersed were Bunny Auchincloss and Kip Perkins, while Isobel von Braun, dressed for bridge, observed the scene like a sullen cobra.

Arthur was also fully attired, wearing a safari suit without necktie. Selena removed her sunglasses in greeting. *"Bon jour, my handsome host."*

He held out his hand and sniffed. "Glad you could make it, Selena. Take off the robe, hop in the pool."

She waved to all. "Alas, darling Isobel and I are safest in bathtubs. But I adore watching others."

She settled herself in a canvas chair facing the swimmers and untied her kaftan to reveal the swimsuit. Then she crossed her legs.

"Zena, get this lady anything she wants to drink."

Selena smiled at the severe servant. "Iced tea, if you please." Then she addressed Isobel's glower. "Kip is so tan! How ever does he manage it?"

The fiancé called, "Heigh ho, Selena Weena."

"I haven't seen you in hours," called Rolf, waist deep in water that dripped from his broad chest.

She recrossed her legs. "I've missed you. And greetings to you, Bunny darling. My, you also have a stunning tan."

"I like your suit," the young woman said.

Not as much as Rolf likes yours, she thought. It was an obscene bikini, a thin strip of red cloth across the hips and a matching bra that bulged with mammaries. Though the actor feigned pleasure disporting with the children, Selena was undeceived. His mind was elsewhere. In his imagination he was ravishing Mrs. Auchincloss.

Why should I feel disappointed Rolf treats me as invisible? she wondered. He's simply my costar; I have no claim on him. Why should I fancy a man with such horrid taste, so easily seduced by an ignorant, common tart?

Meantime, the children won the libertine's attention by climbing on his back. Laughing, he put both hands atop his head and submerged himself, but they held on. When he came up again, comically spewing water, he imitated a bucking bronco. The two passengers screamed and one lost her balance. Reaching to recover it, her tiny fist found his hair and pulled, coming away with his scalp.

Rolf's gasp was simultaneous with Selena's. That beautiful salt-and-pepper hair a *canard*, only a wet wig!

The actor quickly snatched it back and replaced it on the crown of his head, where it sat rakishly askew. Looking to see who might have witnessed this calamity, his eyes came to rest on the woman with the crossed legs.

She donned her sunglasses again, then withered him with a slim smile.

13

SELENA HAD but one live-in servant, the chef Jewel, yet employed a second, a woman named Consuela Gomez. Every letter of reference written on behalf of the cleaning lady made mention of her honesty. If this was intended to mean she could be trusted not to steal, the endorsement was deserved. Unlike some, Consuela never had nor ever would conceal valuables in the portable igloo that contained her lunch.

But she was by nature a curious woman, awed by the lifestyle of her employers and the luxuriousness of their homes compared to her own, a three-room shanty the size of an Elsinore kitchen. Just thirty-nine years old, it was her duty five days a week to babysit six grandchildren, while her husband Diego supported the family as gardener of the retirement community, Casa Feliz. Consuela augmented his earnings by working at Elsinore two days a week; on Tuesdays at Hydrangea, Thursdays at

Versailles. The residences posed different cleaning challenges, the one mostly marble flooring, the other wall-to-wall carpeting; the one requiring a brisk dust mop, the other energetic vacuuming. Both owners were more demanding than Consuela's indolence preferred. Therefore, when safe, she felt no remorse peeking into places she wasn't intended to see, confident hers was an ear attentive to ambush.

This arrogance was punished when twice she was apprehended, once by *Señora* von Braun while examining a Wells Fargo bank statement, again by *Señora* Cabot while reading a love letter pilfered from a yellowing packet.

Both ladies fired her on the spot.

Both recanted and gave her a second chance once they realized the canny Latina might be useful.

This is how Consuela Gomez became a double agent.

"I would never ask you to do anything dishonest, Consuela," *Señora* von Braun said. "I am a deeply religious person opposed to sin in any form, as I know you must be, as a practicing Catholic. But I sometimes worry for my friends, that under certain circumstances the devil may tempt them to stray from the path of righteousness. Therefore, when tidying up Versailles, should you happen to notice anything—oh, unusual, let's say, or out of the ordinary—you may feel safe sharing your concern with me."

And *Señora* Cabot said, "There are people in this club, Consuela, who pretend to be one thing, one kind of person, when in fact they are quite otherwise. I name no names. As a woman of Latin extraction, I know how highly you regard integrity. Therefore, when dusting at Hydrangea, should you stumble upon evidence—not actively seeking it, mind—that something appears to be going on that shouldn't, your observations will be kept absolutely confidential."

Of course, the cleaning lady had yet to master such fluent

English, but by piecing words together she understood she was intended to spy. She shrugged. Maybe, she thought, *las gringas* will pay extra so I can buy gifts for *los niños*.

Though barely two inches taller than five feet, Consuela weighed one hundred and sixty pounds on days she fasted, supplementing a gift for standup. Her stage was a sidewalk in her neighborhood, known as "Little Tijuana," where she entertained an audience seated above on stoops. As she enacted the dowager dialogue, imitating both, their gestures and voices, listeners were splitting their sides.

Kip Perkins was driving Snookums to a hair appointment the day Consuela carried out a thorough search of his room.

As she sorted through women's cosmetics in the man's bathroom—the creams, eye liners, sprays, and perfumes—she felt disgust. But surely, she told herself, *Señora* Cabot must already know about this. I must dig deeper.

So in the bedroom she opened a chest of drawers and felt beneath clothing for anything hidden beneath. In the bottom drawer she panned gold; buried under a pile of sweaters was a collection of pornographic magazines.

Flipping through the pages of one, she said *Ay*! and crossed herself. These photos are different from those Elena showed me in a toilet at Junior High. No women, all men. *Todos*. And what are they doing? It's like a dog fight. *Mira—dos*, now *quatro*, now—*Ay! ocho hombres!* and she crossed herself again.

Consuela considered filching one magazine to show *macho* Diego, but—No, she reminded herself. As the letter says, you are an honest woman; put them back where they came from.

When she described her discovery to *Señora* Cabot, the lady gave a thin smile. "Surely you must be mistaken, Consuela. As you know, Mrs. von Braun is engaged to be married to Mr. Perkins."

Baffled, Consuela sighed, *"Pobrecita."*

When it came *Señora* Cabot's turn to attend the beauty parlor, Consuela ventured into corners of Versailles never explored before. Her quest went unrewarded until, reaching far back in the recesses of the bedroom wardrobe closet, she felt unfamiliar cloth. So she fetched a kitchen flashlight to shine in the dark and discovered another, far different collection.

Choking from mildew, pulling out each, one at a time, she removed a series of what looked like theatrical costumes. She counted thirteen, none similar to any of *Señora* Cabot's everyday wear.

"Why does she keep these things? What would she use them for?" Consuela asked *Señora* von Braun.

The woman narrowed her eyes and stroked her chin. "An intriguing question. Of course, this revelation must go no farther than this room, but I shall need to be exceptionally clever here. I must think of some way to provoke the schemer into providing us an answer."

Consuela held out a hand. Reminded, Isobel removed a five dollar bill from her purse. "I forgot, dear. For your grandchildren."

"Ah, Selena darling!" Isobel called, pausing enroute to the cardroom and a game of bridge. "I hear nothing but rave reports of your performance as Kate; Reggie says he's thrilled to pieces. But tell me—is it customary for an actress to bring her costumes home?"

The hussy appeared confused. "Of course not. My wardrobe stays in the theater where it belongs."

"You wouldn't sneak away a dress or two, for some special occasion?"

Her frown induced a stammer. "No, I—What?—I've—I've absolutely no notion of what you're talking about."

Isobel's laughter resonated in farewell. "If you say so."

✿   ✿   ✿

Reentering Versailles, Selena's legs were atremble. The conversation had been unnerving because von Braun, she knew, was never one to engage in innocent *badinage*. Clearly the villainess knows something, but for the life of me I cannot fathom what it might be.

Costumes.

Suddenly her heart plunged and beat like the wings of a moth. She hurried into her bedroom, opened the door to the wardrobe, and groped as far back to the left as her reach would allow. She made contact with a hanger, lifted it and pulled.

She was holding the nun habit.

I forgot, I forgot! How could I have been so stupid? All these years since Martin died and I never thought to get rid of the costumes!

She sat in the nearest chair to compose herself, her mind flashing back years, recalling she'd married Martin shortly after Laszlo's blowtorch was extinguished. He was an unassuming man, slightly younger than I, but it wasn't true, as gossips insisted, that I married him for the fortune he made manufacturing military uniforms during Viet Nam. No, I was lonely and found him attractive.

It's a short leap from uniforms to costumes, so perhaps I should have been prepared that Martin would have a passion for them. Originally I admit I found it puzzling when he brought home purchases from a store called Free Your Fantasy, all in my size. I soon learned what the naughty man had in mind. It absolutely *inflamed* him to see me dressed as a nun, or an airline stewardess, or a nurse, or a cowgirl, a policewoman, or what have you. Once I surrendered to the spirit of the charade, my theatrical background came in handy. I became superbly skilled, if I do say so myself, at enacting delicious improvisations, often with imaginative props.

Ah, Martin! I weep to recall your final night on this earth. I was wearing perhaps your favorite, the girl scout costume, the one with a special collar to receive merit badges you awarded for outstanding services.

I remember I'd just straddled your love dart; you were in the act of pinning a badge to my collar, grunting with passion, when abruptly the grunting turned to ghastly gargling. I looked down to see your eyes had rolled to the back of your head, gazing at God.

Oh Martin, Martin! Please forgive me. I never expected my weapon of destruction would claim you, too!

Holding the nun habit, wiping away a tear, Selena offered a silent prayer. Oh God, if You do exist, if there is indeed a heaven, please, please find a place for my Martin. Perhaps as manager of Only Angels Have Wings?

A thought crossed my mind to be rejected instantly. No, I can never contribute these garments to the Romero Players. Absolutely not. Instead, I shall have them boxed and burned.

AROUND THE BLOCK

Caitlin Wills

One of my informants tells me rehearsals for "Kiss Me Kate" are so exciting, even members of the chorus linger to witness staging of the numbers.

The choreographer, **Velvet Jackson**, has her own nightclub here in Loma Bella, as well as a dance studio, and word is her tutelage has energized the entire company.

I'm told that equally exciting are the sparks generated by costars **Selena Cabot** and **Rolf Victor**, fire sufficient to ignite a summer barbeque. As it happens, readers, neither is married!

The music is being created exclusively by **Elizabeth Clarke** (formerly **Tallmadge**), whose artistry supports the fine singing voices of the stars.

Romero director **Reggie Burbage** reminds us it's only two weeks to opening night!

On occasion Caitlin Wills wore spectacles. She did this to give herself a more severe appearance, one to ensure she'd be taken seriously. Together with a habitual frown, the affectation was intended to distract attention from her sightliness, the close-cropped reddish hair and trim figure. She needn't have troubled. By itself, her aggressive demeanor was a turn-off.

Caitlin Mahoney was educated first at a San Rafael convent, then at Northwestern's School of Journalism, which landed her a job at the San Francisco *Examiner*, where she met reporter Dermot Wills, had his baby, and raised it as a working mom.

As he walked out the door, out of her life, Wills said, "You know, Caitlin, you're a lousy reporter because you don't listen; you're too busy bitching and whining about something. What you should be is a critic."

And her editor agreed.

Caitlin was at first mystified, then outraged when deposed as drama critic of the Loma Bella *Sun*, just because she'd written the truth about an appalling interpretation of Tennessee Williams. On the *Examiner* she'd been given freedom to write candidly, even when her opinion was unpopular, but her editors in this cultural backwater were browbeaten by wealthy advertisers, like the wife of ham actor Reggie Burbage.

In fairness, when approached the woman admitted responsibility.

"Sorry about that, Ms. Wills," said Daisy. "No hard feelin's. The wellbein' of the Romero depends on media support."

Well, such a rationale was so disgraceful Caitlin was tempted to resign from the paper altogether, then remembered deadbeat Dermot contributed nothing to the support of their teenaged daughter. She needed the work.

Grudgingly she accepted a substitute sweetmeat, as society columnist. She caved in because hers was an assignment so mindlessly simple it was almost shaming to collect her salary.

On the minus side of the ledger, it was necessary, of course, to attend the parties she wrote about, necessary to put on a friendly face for guests transparently currying her favor. Memorizing their names was unrequired because the hostess always provided a guest list, so all she had to remember was to type them in bold font for easy ego-enhancement. And the paper also provided her with a photographer, Dennis San Miguel, whose ponytail was socially unacceptable, but whose charm convinced people to pose in self-conscious groupings, smiles focused on his lens.

Otherwise she listened for inane comments that might lend a particular flavor to a particular event, careful to plug the charity that was ostensible reason for the affair, when in truth it was little more than an excuse for wealthy women to flaunt a new frock or jewelry.

Husbands paid for their wives' philanthropy twice. First by writing a check. Then by trussing themselves in tuxedos to perform duty dances. Little wonder the men drank so heavily.

These parties were so insular, so silly, it got Caitlin's Irish up. She once confronted Isobel von Braun. "Have you no interests in life beyond Elsinore? Are you not aware there's a real world out there, where many people live in poverty, where prejudice exists, where every day there are victims of violence?"

The woman was untroubled. "Well yes, dear, of course. But those problems are being attended to nicely by our wonderful President Bush——the younger, I mean—so no reason to fret."

The columnist persisted. "But why don't you get involved? Here you have all the money in the world and do nothing."

Isobel's eyebrows levitated. "You are misinformed, dear; facts are facts. Each year Loma Bella charities distribute thousands of dollars to thousands of the needy."

Why waste my breath? Wills asked herself. Why not expose this superficial nonsense by writing about it instead? It'll make a helluva book. So keep your ear to the ground, old girl, and fill your notebook with tasty particulars.

Like the Paradise Beach controversy. Caitlin learned certain Loma Bellans were critical of the Loma Bella Police Department for its negligence in protecting the cove from an incursion of nudists. Retired Judge Horace Tallmadge wrote a scathing letter published in the *Sun* that caused Chief Chuck Mooney to dispatch a weekend foot patrol to serve citations. But enforcement was pointless because many sunbathers came from out of town and would never pay the fine, and Mooney had more urgent priorities—crimes, not misdemeanors. Accordingly, the following weekend Paradise Lost became Paradise Regained.

I don't understand why the Judge is in such high dudgeon, Caitlin thought. He's not risking skin cancer. And you can bet your sun block no self-respecting member of the Elsinore Country Club would be caught dead down there.

This, Caitlin decided, is just the sort of stuff I need for my book, so why not make a field trip?

She chose a Saturday. Not knowing the location of the cove's access from a cliff above, she set off in search of Paradise from the shore, from nearby Marvista Hotel, wearing a floppy hat and slacks to protect her fair skin. Where sand turned to rocks, she rolled up her slacks to the knee, removed her sandals, and stepped into ankle-deep rushing water, a refreshing remedy to the noonday sun. After stepping cautiously over stones she soon emerged onto another beach. Still carrying the sandals, she avoided scalding sand to proceed at the ocean's edge, advancing toward an assemblage of mixed brown, pink, white, and black flesh.

She approached the nudists tactfully, courteously averting her eyes, until splashed by a group of worshippers frolicking in the surf. For a moment she thought she recognized a slim girl flipping a Frisbee at a young man. But it couldn't be—no. But it was!

"Daphne!" she screamed. The product of her womb, dressed as she was the morning of her entrance into life. And in the company of the forbidden biker, Gonzo!

"Mother!" Daphne screamed in return, and ran to collect her clothing balled on a blanket. Caitlin scuttled after her, sputtering fury, and was reaching to grab her daughter's arm when she tripped over a naked male. "I beg your pardon," she mumbled. "Ms. Wills!" cried Isobel von Braun's alarmed fiancé, flopping over to bury his face in the sand.

"Oh my God, my God!" the columnist wailed, yielding to tears. She rose to her feet, brushing sand from her knees.

"Jesus!" Daphne cried.

"I'm outa here!" yelled a dripping Gonzo, scooping up his clothing and sprinting for the cliff.

Beneath her Robin Perkins was whimpering. "Oh, please. You didn't see me, did you? I'm not here. Please?"

When gossip columnist Caitlin Wills requested permission to observe a runthrough of the musical, Reggie had grudgingly agreed, but here it was fifteen minutes past the appointed hour and she was a no-show.

Deucedly impolite of the woman, he thought, and clapped his hands for the company's attention. "All right, children, let's take it from Baptista's opening entrance."

As Lord Peter hooked arms with Selena and Bunny, the director made a belated discovery—the man was wearing spectacles! "Oh good heavens. It's my fault, Lord Peter, for not having said something sooner. Completely escaped my attention, I fear. Sorry, but you must dispense with your glasses."

"Dispense with them? Without them I can't see; I'm a blind man."

"But people of that period had no glasses, don't you know. They didn't exist. They simply had to make do."

"How am I to make do? If I can't see I'll be crashing into people and furniture."

Reggie tried his disarming chuckle. "Nonsense, old fellow; indulge me, if you please. Allow me to hold the spectacles and let's try this opening entrance where you address Kip and the other suitors." He put the glasses aside to clap hands again. "Everyone, places please...Begin."

A squinting Lord Peter grasped an arm of each daughter and was towed onstage, saying,

"'Gentlemen, importune me no further,

For how I firmly am resolved you know—'"

"Where is he? Which one is Gremio?"

"Here, Lord Peter. I'm over here."

"Ah. And Lucentio?"

"Behind you, sir," said Kip.

The actor flapped his arms in frustration. "You see what I mean, Reggie? For heaven's sake, I'm talking to ghosts; it's no good. Better that I withdraw from the play."

At such a late date this would be calamitous, so Reggie scuttled to improvise. "No, no, inconceivable. We'll—we'll—I know. Contact lenses. How about contact lenses, Lord Peter? Ever worn them?"

"No, I've never had the need. Until now."

Reggie called, "Daisy, precious producer, would you make an appointment for Lord Peter to see an ophthalmologist? Tomorrow, hopefully?"

His wife shook her head adamantly. "The budget doesn't cover medical expenses, Reg."

"It does now, darling. Don't forget, we don't have understudies, do we? If someone fell ill, we'd simply have to cancel the performance and return the price of the tickets. No no, my love, I'd like Lord Glenn to see an eye specialist first thing in the morning."

At Monday's rehearsal Baptista reported for duty without spectacles but with his eyes leaking tears. "What ho," Reggie greeted him. "I'm looking at a new man."

"I think I'm allergic to these damned things," Glenn complained.

"You'll get used to them, old haggis," the director said cheerfully. "Every new experience takes a bit of getting used to."

Lord Peter used a finger to wipe the moisture beneath his left eye. "I'm not so sure—" he began, then yelled, "Ah! Holy sh—I mean, Godfrey Daniel! Now I've done it! The damned lens has popped out!"

"Hold it, everyone!" Reggie ordered. "For heaven's sake, hold it, stand perfectly still. We mustn't risk stepping on it. Let's all just look, first of all, shall we?…Does anyone see it anywhere on the floor?"

The cast stood in concentrated silence before Bunny said, "No. Shouldn't we kind of squat in place, sort of feel around the floor?"

"Good idea," said Kip.

Everybody squatted and searched a full circle of surrounding space.

"This stage has never been dusted," Selena griped.

"Any luck?" Lord Peter called petulantly, irritated by his blunder.

"Not yet," said Reggie. "Patience, everyone."

Buster Rooney said, "Maybe it bounced to another part of the stage."

Minutes passed, the only sound that of hands sweeping wood.

At last Rolf had had enough. Standing, he said, "This is ridiculous—grown people playing blind man's buff. God's sake, Reg, buy him another set." He took a step forward and all heard a small snap.

The company groaned in unison.

Lord Peter was disgusted. Fishing out the second contact, he threw it to the floor. "That's it. So much for contact lenses. I've had it, Reggie. If you want me to perform in this burlesque, it's spectacles or another actor."

"But people didn't wear—"

"I know, I know—"

"The audience will find your character unbelievable—"

"So what? Screw it! Who's to care? Maybe Baptista was a man before his time." Holding out a palm, he said, "If you'll be so kind, give me back my specs."

Sighing, Reggie returned them.

Lord Peter put them on and looked around. "Wow. The gang's all here. Nice seeing you folks again."

14

BAPTISTA GLENN made certain his golf bag was buckled securely to the back of the cart, seated himself at the wheel, then drove to where Tisdale, Clarke, and Trevor Faye had assembled on the first tee.

This is one game I don't look forward to, he thought, but what the hell. It couldn't have been easy for Selena Cabot to beg; surely she knows her brother's chances of membership are slim and none.

"I realize it's important he golf with important members," she said, "in hopes they'll be impressed enough to support his candidacy. May I impose on you, dear friend, to arrange a game?"

You don't say no to Louise's best friend. I hear the same stories everyone else does about Hugh Tisdale's sexcapades, but maybe they're exaggerated. I can only tell you I've played with the guy twice and recall just two things—he's a terrible golfer with a terrible temper.

"Top of the morning to you, gentlemen." I lifted a scorecard clamped to the steering wheel, holes already circled according to handicap, and walked to the tee. "Let me be sure I have this right—Trevor, you bandit, you're a 2?"

The lush grunted assent, clearly distrusting his diction at nine in the morning. He was weaving in place, supported by his driver.

It's galling, Glenn thought. Here's this man, utterly nondescript were it not for his fluid swing, a sot who never practices, who's never sure what hole he's playing, who keeps his buzz by refreshing himself from a thermos in his cart. How in hell does he manage to shoot below par?

"Baxter and Hugh, you may be Gangsters on the stage, but kindly do not pick my pocket on the golf course. Baxter, I have you as a 19. Am I right?"

"Sure, and you're a 16. I looked it up."

I did some checking, too. Thank God he wasn't wearing one of his Speedos. He was so ill at ease in shorts, he fidgeted as though fire ants infested his crotch.

"And Hugh, it says here you're a 24?"

"Yup."

I know a lie when I hear one, but I let it pass.

Tisdale was also wearing shorts, a poor choice for a bow-legged man.

I threw a tee onto the grass. It pointed to Faye. "Your team has honors, Trev. Go easy on us. Louise says I better not lose more than an Abraham Lincoln."

Faye stood unsteadily over his ball before smoking it two hundred and seventy yards straight down the middle. His partner,

Tisdale, wiggled and waggled, huffed and puffed, before topping his drive seventeen inches off the tee.

"Well, it's straight," Clarke chortled.

On the next hole, I noticed Tisdale pretend to find his ball in a cluster of trees when in fact it was lost.

On number Three he used a shoe to kick his shot clear from where it was snared in a nest of twigs.

On number Five, bunkered in a trap so deep he thought he was invisible, he used one hand to throw a spray of sand, the other to loft his ball back on the fairway.

Yet thanks to Trevor Faye, after eight holes the match was dead even.

Then, on the ninth tee, Tisdale hit a snap hook so ugly it landed on the patio of Bulls and Bears, ricocheted off the tile, bounced off the roof, and plopped in the deep end of the swimming pool.

Frustrated beyond measure, Selena's brother screamed a word never spoken aloud at Elsinore, a word used by the vulgar to describe copulation. Its echo was lingering in the crisp morning air when he took his club by the handle, whirled it around his head like a mace, and flung it as far he could.

It was his longest shot of the day, as high as it was long. The club came to rest tangled in high tension wires that provided power to all of Elsinore, sending off a shower of sparks.

Arthur Auchincloss was seated at his computer when it went down, erasing important investment data he'd neglected to save.

Bulldog Jarvis's security screen sighed and died.

Chef Luigi's luncheon special of the day, canelloni, sizzled in darkness, burned beyond redemption before he found a flashlight.

Consuela Gomez was trapped whilst snooping in *Senora* von Braun's wardrobe closet. Disoriented, she reached about wildly, grabbing so much clothing the rod snapped, burying her in silks and satins.

Judge Horace Tallmadge had just enjoyed his most satisfactory bowel movement in weeks, and was bending to pull up his trousers when plunged into an abyss that pitched him forward, to strike his head on the bathroom scales.

At Hydrangea, Kip had been watching a tape of "All My Children" with Bunny and Rolf Victor when the screen's image flickered and disappeared. In unison all three rose. Rolf was groping to locate the door knob when his hand accidentally manipulated one of Bunny's breasts. She yipped and delivered a blind roundhouse right that caught Kip flush on the temple, dropping him like a stone.

Worst, the outage short-circuited every security alarm in Elsinore, a cacophony of dissimilar bells. The racket was amplified by the arrival of two fire trucks, sirens shrilling, lights spinning. And much to the mortification of Bulldog, the firefighters were followed in turn by three black and whites, Cuffs Mooney in the van.

They were too late to extinguish the fires remaining in Hugh Tisdale; he'd stormed directly from the ninth tee to the clubhouse in search of Otto. Flinging open a doorway to darkness, he paused, then shouted furious complaint into the void.

"Can anybody in charge of this club explain to me why a moron was authorized to string a power line lower than a snake's hip? You incompetents will be hearing from my attorney. It's an effing disgrace!"

Power was not restored until late afternoon, in time for Elsinore wives—more often their servants—to prepare the evening meal.

Reggie sat down to dinner with Daisy in Wilde House to share continuing concerns. "Do your realize we're just days away from dress rehearsal? The thought makes me ill."

"No need to fret, dear. Thanks to your trademark charm, you've recruited the best people possible, both in front of the footlights and behind. Now pick up your fork."

Complying, Reggie sighed. "I'm comfortable with my principals, or at least three of them. Victor and Cabot sing beautifully. Bunny Auchincloss is a disgraceful scene-stealer with equal skills in song and dance. But what am I do with the fourth? Kip Perkins was lumbered on me because, for whatever reason, he was itching to play Bill Calhoun. Doesn't the fellow realize he's a disaster? He sings passably but dances poorly—not even our superb choreographer can save him. Not that Kippy isn't trying. On the contrary, he tries terribly hard; too terribly hard."

"Perhaps, dear," said Daisy, "you could convince Isobel it'd be kinder for her fiancé to sit this one out."

"Too late! I might have tried earlier, but she's the purse strings, isn't she? Oh, I realize I could lean on you for money if necessary, but Isobel's support of this production is symbolic of an entire community's affection for the Romero."

"Eat your veggies, Reg; no need to become agitated. I'm sure the rest of the actors will be fine."

Reggie used a napkin to wipe the taste of anxiety from his lips. "Not the rest, just a few. Lord Peter Glenn has so little to do he can't be a liability. Both Baxter Clarke and Hugh Tisdale are having a lark doing the Gangsters. And I'm sure audiences will explode with laughter when they recognize their police chief, Chuck Mooney, playing a dancing doorman. But!"

"The succotash is gettin' cold, dear. Have a sip of wine and calm yourself."

"But it was stupid of me to have cast Arthur Auchincloss. I only did it to please Bunny, and what's it gotten me? The man's an absolute stick, so wooden you can strike a match on him. And the most talented player of all, my beloved Mary Tallmadge, has chosen to portray a stage manager. What an awful waste!"

Daisy sat back in her chair. "Reginald Burbage, you just stop now; it's not like you to dwell on the negative. The cast will respond to your superb direction as it always does. In fact, if I may say so, dear, some believe you're an even better director than you are an actor. And you know how people feel about your actin'."

Reggie inhaled the adulation. "Yes, yes. You're right as always, old cabbage. Forgive my doubts."

Daisy returned to the plate. "Yes, the cast'll be fine, but I must voice a few doubts about our production team, beginnin' with myself. You may not realize it, dear, but you tend to be less patient with me than others. I never wanted anythin' to do with props, and here I am, pushin' this cumbersome trolley with all those drawers, and though I've tried to organize which should be where, if I'm lookin' for a pillow, I'm as apt to find a magazine, or a pewter mug when I want an artificial rose."

Her husband smiled encouragement. "You've plenty of time to get it right, darling."

"Have you forgotten the runthrough when I forgot to include the note with Selena's bouquet? Poor Rolf was grabbin' at air and Selena had to turn her back, pretendin' to stuff it down her front."

Reg waved away the recollection. "A one-time slip, dearest."

"And you know how clumsy I am," she whined. "You know my history of bein' accident-prone. I worry I could cause clatter that might drown out the music."

Reggie dismissed this firmly. "I have the utmost confidence in you, precious. You're my backstage star."

Daisy would not be mollified. "May I ask you a rude question, Reg? Why have you placed Judge Horace Tallmadge in charge of sound? He's eighty-seven years old and deaf as a post."

The director coughed. "Well—well, Mary implored me to

give him something to do. I couldn't very well assign him a job that demands readiness, could I? He really rather enjoys himself, playing with the telephone, crash box, and siren. Yesterday I shouted how much I'm relying on him, and he shouted back he won't let me down. Of course, our safeguard here is young Buster, who'll cue him with hand signals and even prod the man if necessary."

"Speakin' of whom, darlin'," Daisy continued. "Buster does all the work. It's the stage manager's job to stand offstage holdin' the prompt book, but Kenneth Holly does nothin' but sniff around the chorus girls. He's a lecher and a loafer. Why not fire him?"

Reggie threw up his hands. "He's given me no cause. He contributes by pulling the curtain. Besides, if I were to cashier all the men in the company who're sexually hyperactive there'd be no show."

She held up a hand. "One more question, Reg, and then I'm done with the naysayin'. Just what makes Lady Louise Glenn qualified to run the wardrobe department?"

The question induced another cough. "Well—well, Selena begged me to include her. They're best friends, after all, and you like to make your star happy. I know she has taste—you can see that in how she dresses—"

"Does she know how to sew?"

Reggie gargled before saying, "Well, I would imagine. The job's uncomplicated, after all. It only involves being certain the proper costumes are hanging in the proper dressing rooms, and every few days remembering to collect them for laundering."

Daisy raised her arms in surrender. "Who am I to quibble? You've made chicken salad out of chicken feathers before."

"One moment, if you please." Reggie sat puffed as a pigeon. "Don't I deserve praise for my other choices? Morgan Ball has designed wonderfully practical sets, has she not? She's assembled a crew of efficient, amazingly strong women. It's true Seymour Katz's lighting aptitude was learned in high school theater, but he's already pre-set dimmers on his lighting board. And just try to find anything negative to say about my musical director! Libby Clarke labors harder than a wetback, banging away on the rented Steinway. Her 'orchestra pit' is tinier than my closet and so close to the footlights the heat must be stifling. Yet do you ever hear her complain? Never!"

"Sorry, Reg. I'll shut up."

"What I am saying, my love, is our glass is three-quarters full." He raised his wine to demonstrate the amount. "Let us rejoice!"

15

IN THE CALM of her dressing room Selena prepared herself for battle.

She addressed her image in the wall mirror: Twinkle, twinkle, little star. It's dress rehearsal.

Then she adjusted the magnified mirror for closeup inspection of her handiwork: Eye liner, fine. Lipstick, okay. She used tissue to blot the lips, then removed the tissue around her neck that protected the wardrobe. She was set for action.

The parallels are spooky, she thought. Vanessi's scared because she hasn't appeared on a stage in years, and Cabot's just as petrified. My God, what have I done, thinking I could recapture the magic enjoyed briefly in my twenties? Reggie lavishes me with compliments and Rolf is equally supportive, but are they sincere?

Too late, mate. Over fifty people are counting on you.

The rap at the door admitted lovable Buster. "Five minutes,

Ms. Cabot," and the door remained ajar for Rolf to intrude himself. Embracing her from behind he carefully kissed her hair. "*Merde*, my lady."

She patted his hands. "Break a leg."

"We'll kill 'em. Tell me again—I'm in denial—just who are these folks Reggie's invited to test us?"

"They're all students from UCLB."

Rolf groaned. "Oh God, infantile critics. Get ready for laughs in all the wrong places." She was unsuccessful concealing a tremor in her left hand. Her costar grasped it, saying, "Selena, you are dynamite. Dy-no-mite. You're not just talented, you're so sexy that if I were ten years younger I'd put a move on you."

As planned, he'd coaxed a laugh. "Be careful. I can be dangerous." The statement induced flashback quickly blinked away. "See you out there in No Man's Land."

She stood, flicked powder off her first change, the summer dress, adjusted the pearls at her throat, breathed deeply, then strode out the door to another, the one through which she would make her first entrance. She'd never approved of actors who peer out at the audience, counting the house or looking for familiar faces. This was a moment to summon concentration.

Buster was at the elbow of Seymour Katz, seated at his lighting board. Looking at his watch, the boy instructed, "Take the house to half."

The buzz of conversation out front subsided, replaced by a few coughs. At an opposite backstage station Ken Holly stood ready to raise the curtain, awaiting the signal of his young assistant. The boy consulted his prompt book and pointed to Libby in the orchestra pit. "Cue overture." Hearing the piano chords, he touched Seymour's shoulder. "House out." Then he pointed to Holly. "And—curtain."

To reveal the milling chorus as they celebrate "Another Op'nin', Another Show." Selena was third in line. Kip was first to enter and, repeating a habitual gaffe, he tripped on the door strip and catapulted onstage. Uncertain whether or not this was intended, the audience dismissed his approach, already enamored of Bunny, who succeeded him. Then came Selena's moment. No acting was required to express enchantment; the footlights invited her downstage center where she felt herself bathed in isolated illumination. Looking out at the audience she was reminded they were, collectively, a restive animal that could turn dangerous unless tamed. The front rows were painted gold by the lights, waning to shades of gray, ebbing to total darkness.

As staged, Selena seated herself on a chair, listening to the singing. My turn will come soon enough, she thought, and then Rolf entered, clapping hands for attention. "All right, company! Thank you!"

And we're off and running—to God knows where.

Reggie stood at the back of the house, prepared to take notes by penlight. It was impossible to total just how many dress rehearsals he'd experienced in a lifetime, but as actor and director he reckoned they numbered in the hundreds. Dress rehearsal was a ritual bloodletting that confirmed how little previous rehearsals had actually accomplished.

The audience, admitted for free, were stern critics notwithstanding; on occasion, merciless. Reggie had deliberately invited college students because they were likely to pounce on mistakes like hyenas on a wounded zebra. His cast had been a bit too cocksure for Reg's taste, and tonight's ordeal might reclaim their attention.

His pen had noted a few minor errors, including Kip's stumbling entrance, when the first catastrophe occurred. During Selena's singing of "So In Love" there was a reverberating crash from offstage, followed by a female cry of "Ow!" Since the sounds emanated from the area near the prop trolley, it was safe to assume Daisy had pulled out a drawer too far.

The audience loved it, applauding as they would a waiter who'd dropped a tray.

Reggie suffered their derision quietly. He made no note. It was his fault, actually, insisting his accident-prone wife be put in charge of objects. He could be sure she'd remind him later that the fault was his, not hers.

Catastrophe number two occurred in the scene where the Gangsters come to collect on Rolf's IOU, when half of Hugh Tisdale's mustache fell off. He reached down to retrieve it, pressed it back in place, and it fell off again. This time he let it lie on the floor and put a hand over his mouth, even when speaking.

A heckler called, "Hey, buddy—your dentist give you Novocain?"

Reggie made a note to have a word with makeup person Mary.

Catastrophe number three occurred during the "Tom, Dick or Harry" number, when Kip Perkins danced so energetically he split the seat of his trousers. He was the last person to notice the cleft and must have been puzzled by a swelling buzz from the audience as students took turns pointing out the gaposis. When Kip felt air where his seat should be, he went to the nearest wall and danced in place.

Reggie made a note to have a word with Lady Louise.

Catastrophe number four occurred when Selena was placing a phone call to General Harrison Howell for help. As she was speaking into the instrument the phone rang. Gallant Selena ignored the mystery, but then the phone rang again!

A student shouted, "It's for you, lady!", precipitating a gale of laughter.

Reggie was furious. Who cued the codger? Buster? How could Mary have been so inattentive?

At intermission he stuffed his notebook in his pocket and

hurried from the theater to separate himself from embarrassment. He went straight to the nearby cocktail lounge, the Green Room, the site Buster Rooney routinely searched for absent actors, ordered himself a stiff shot of Glenlivet, and masochistically savored the burning in his chest. Looking up, he saw Trevor Faye lifting his glass in a silent toast. The rascal should have been seated in the box office!

Surely, Reggie thought as he positioned himself to witness Act Two, nothing worse can happen. Then he contradicted himself. When will I learn? Worse has a habit of becoming worst.

And sure enough, humiliation awaited, administered by the person I should never have cast in the first, second, or third place, Arthur Auchincloss. A prolonged stage silence captured my attention. Looking, it was obvious General Howell had dried. His growling and harrumphing was plea for a cue.

Rewinding my mental tape to previous dialogue, I recalled Rolf teasing the man, asking, "Women should be struck regularly, like gongs?"

And I recalled hearing Arthur's reply, "Who said that?"

"Noel Coward."

"Now there's a man I'd like to meet," Auchincloss said, clean forgetting the second part of his line, the joke.

In pity's name, where's Buster? Then I heard his loud whisper. "A straight talker."

The drowning man evidently hadn't heard, so Buster repeated the cue louder.

Still the actor hadn't heard. Defenseless, he called "What?"

This time Buster used full voice, to no avail.

Auchincloss had run out of patience. He shouted, "*What?*" Thank God for experienced assistance. Rolf Victor took over, nudging the actor's memory by speaking the words Auchincloss should have been speaking. "General," he said, "I'll bet the reason you'd want to meet Coward is because he's a straight talker. But I'd have to tell you, sir. Not exactly."

The ruse failed to fool the hyenas. They howled with glee, not at
the belated joke but at the blunder, rewarding it with cheers.

Next morning Reggie addressed a chastened company. Smiling
to put a good face on it, he said, "Children, it's the oldest adage
in show business, you know. 'Bad dress rehearsal means outstanding opening night.' I am not going to insist we rehearse all
the horrid moments that transpired last night in order to correct
them. No, I consider them an aberration. Instead I am going to
give everyone the day off to rest, recuperate, and prepare for
what I predict will be a stunning effort from cast and crew alike.
Bless you all."

Midafternoon, Selena opened the unlocked dressing room door
of her costar. She wanted to leave him a present, a time-hon-
ored opening night tradition. She considered giving him a ster-
ling silver picture frame with his initials, but realized this would
be as unsuitable for Rolf as it would for her. Neither had a face
to honor there—not a husband, not a wife or children, not even
pets. Their dressing tables were bare except for flowers and
messages sent by thoughtful friends.

Selena set down a gift-wrapped package ordered from a luggage store in Beverly Hills. It was a script binder of Corinthian
leather with the letters "RV" embossed in the lower right-hand
corner. Her note read: "Your affectionate support of this musical wannabe has meant more than I can ever tell you. You are
my Victor always. S."

Rolf sneaked into Selena's dressing room an hour later, placing a
gift-wrapped parcel under the mirror. He'd had difficulty locat-
ing something so specifically uncommon, yet succeeded at a
sacrifice of time and money. It was a Cole Porter songbook dat-
ed 1935, with inky changes to words and lyrics, slashes and
scratches in the handwriting of the genius himself. His note

read: "Thine is that special face, thine that special talent to bur-
nish a rusty star. I thank you, beautiful lady. R."

Standing once again at the rear of his Romero theater, Reggie
Burbage was taut with apprehension, dreading a repetiton of
last night's debacle.

Relax, old fellow, he told himself—there's absolutely nothing
you can do. Who knows better than you the stage is the actor's
medium? Once the curtain rises a director is helpless; the cast
will either perform as intended or they will not.

So he lifted rigid elbows from the back row and flapped his
arms, ordering them to loosen up. The curtain rose to find him
so intent doing relaxation exercises he could not have told you
how the first act was going. The stiff drinks he'd imbibed at dinner did double service.

At intermission he visited the Green Room for added seda-
tion. Out of superstition, he refrained from mingling with the
audience, instead crossing the street to stare at newspapers in
the vending machines outside the post office. The mixed babble
of male and female voices told him nothing.

When he saw first-nighters return through the oak doors, he
returned as well, this time only to listen. He stood with eyes
closed, half-hearing the music and dialogue, surrendering to
conscious sleep. Physically and mentally he occupied a canoe
being washed downstream, enjoying scenic particulars, his des-
tination unknown, at peace with nature and himself.

Reggie wakened to an explosion of applause. It was the final
curtain, he realized, and he was astonished to feel his cheeks
awash with tears. He was the proud father of an overachieving
family, a company that had performed to perfection. Everything
that had previously gone wrong, tonight had miraculously gone
right.

His pair of hands joined six hundred and twenty-five others
in appreciation. When Kip stepped forward for his curtain call

the bow was received warmly, but when Bunny stepped forward the audience rose to its feet and cheered, a cheering that, at the appearance of Selena and Rolf, swelled to a tempest of love, acclaim that reverberated from walls and ceiling.

The director allowed his tears to flow unabated. He'd created a hit.

Isobel had rented the Café Hermosa for an opening night party. The restaurant was just four blocks from the Romero, easy walking distance. The excitement of theatergoers suggested Sardi's, the Broadway restaurant where spectators could mingle with cast members as they awaited early newspaper editions in an atmosphere of nervous expectancy. What would the critics' verdict be?

Of course, there would be no early edition in Loma Bella; it would be two days before people learned the opinion of Felix Zellner, current critic of the *Sun*. However, the former critic, Caitlin Wills, was present at the Hermosa, taking notes and instructing her photographer, pony-tailed Dennis San Miguel, where to point his lens.

When the hostess embraced fiancé Kip, she wept a mixture of relief and delight. "To think you had all this talent and I never realized!" She pinched his cheek. "You gifted little tyke!" Then Isobel went to Selena and gently pulled her away from a huddle of admirers. Embracing the actress, bestowing air kisses at both cheeks, she cried, "Never again will I question how you spent your early years. Never! What a glorious voice!"

The Wills woman intruded. "Could we get a shot of you two, patroness and star?"

Selena laughed. "Sure. Let's do it, Isobel."

Before she could protest Isobel felt her arm being uplifted, fingers interlaced with Selena's, an Olympic victory posture. The flash bulb winked, preserving for posterity smiles of immortal friendship.

AROUND THE BLOCK
Caitlin Wills

The verdict is in!

For you readers who may have missed the review of *Kiss Me Kate* by my colleague Felix Zellner in yesterday's *Sun* I quote in part:

"**Reggie Burbage** has pulled off a coup. Venturing into territory no Romero production has visited before, the director and his producer wife have added musical theater to the dossier of their achievements.

"It is with absolute candor that I tell you **Selena Cabot** has a singing voice and stage presence to match that of guest star **Rolf Victor**. The pair are brilliant. **Bunny Auchincloss** is a show-stopper as Bianca, and a surprisingly good turn is contributed by **Robin Perkins** as Lucentio.

"Momentarily I was confused by **Lord Peter Glenn**'s use of spectacles as Baptista, until I realized he was making a character statement. He perceived the period's pretense to be sham.

"No fooling, cross-my-heart, this is a must-see entertainment certain to delight audiences throughout its run.

"And in closing, a critic would be remiss if he failed to mention that **Elizabeth Clarke** fills a piano bench with generous virtuosity."

16

ROLF REQUESTED that Kip drive him to the theater an hour before curtain so he could vocalize. It'd be inconsiderate to do scales in Isobel's home, where neighbors might complain. Which caused him to wonder, when do you suppose Selena does her exercises? Maybe that mansion has a soundproof room.

He encouraged Kip to vocalize as well. The young man took his stage responsibilities seriously and it showed; his performance improved by the night.

Then it was on to makeup and a routine so familiar he could do it in the dark. Simple pancake base spread with a sponge. White brushed under the eyes to minimize those desks under the pupils. Dark pencil drawn under the lower lashes. Subtle rouge to highlight the cheekbones. And last, the hair.

Ah, the hair. Only Selena knows my secret, he thought, and she's too much a lady to noise it around that I wear a toupée. Still, you gotta admit it's a first-class rug; it should be, for what it cost. It requires care and feeding, of course. I begin by combing out the salt-and-pepper hairs so they look casually tousled, then I apply glue to the lace, center the piece, set the hair spray on Super-hold to fire off a cloud of sweet-smelling mist, press the edges to be sure no glue's in evidence, and *voilà*!

You're looking at a leading man.

As *Kate* settled into its run, rehearsals over and done, Rolf Victor had unwelcome leisure to ruminate on the past. In my prime, he reflected, my looks and charm, or what one woman called my "lazy insolence," attracted females like bees to a honeycomb. Beginning with divorced Brenda, the bedroom holocaust who paid for all the acting and singing lessons. But I had to get careless, didn't I? Naturally she dumped me after catching me in the sack with her teenaged daughter.

Strange but true—somehow I've never had to advertise it—for me lovemaking's a skill Stanislavsky never taught, and even now, because I keep in shape and watch my diet, older women suspect I still make beautiful music.

But the key word here is "older." In bygone days I was beating young women away with my script—they couldn't get enough of me. Oh, there were some who called me a prick because I kissed and ran, but it wasn't as if I lacked morals. Just the opposite. I made it a strict rule: no married women, and I never broke my word. I defy you: name me a time I propositioned a married woman. So in my mind I was never a prick. I mean, I've never hurt anybody who wasn't looking to get hurt.

And what about the time *I* got hurt, when Faith left her wedding ring on the bedside table so she could screw other guys with a clear conscience?

Turnabout's fair play, Rolfie.

Okay. But now—today, after fifty-nine years—the popsicles who give me lover's nuts look straight through me, like I'm a has-been more to be pitied than desired. A case in point, Bunny Auchincloss, a fantasy to keep a man awake nights. Can't she see I'm a better deal than her husband, the nerd with the big nose?

Guess not. So it turns out schmoozing Bunny's buddy Kip was a waste of time.

Well, hell, he's nice enough. I've always hit it off with homos because I don't knock their lifestyle. But using the word "gay"? I choke whenever I try it. Once upon a time it was an adjective that meant indescribably happy. Now, I ask you, how many indescribably happy homosexuals have you ever met? How about none? But I'll be honest—in the past I sought them out for the fringe benefits, because women are drawn like fireflies to unthreatening men.

Unthreatening, I admit, is an adjective never squandered on me.

So I suppose it's back to the golden oldies. I'll admit it, Selena Cabot's been growing on me. She's got those great legs and a sassy side that dares you to prove you can keep up with her in the hay.

I've been thinking: I just may accept the challenge.

Elsinore women who congregated under driers at Wesley's Salon included Selena Cabot. The hairdresser was delighted to abet her appearance as Kate by cropping her raven hair to allow more freedom dancing, and he applied a subtle tint to preserve its beauty. Selena adored Wesley and vice versa; the two loved sharing wicked whispers. Therefore she was torn following the incident at the Auchincloss swimming pool, tempted to tattle, yet in the end guardian of Rolf's reputation.

So she sat mute in Wesley's Salon, absorbing the boy's chit-chat during the wash and set: Daisy Burbage had again demonstrated Iowa taste by selling property to a fish merchant. Morgan Ball had been seen holding hands with the Homecoming Queen of Loma Bella High. Ashley Faye's efforts to save a Saint Cecilia marriage had failed because both parties had misrepresented themselves—the husband as descendant of the House of Hohenzollern, the wife as illegitimate issue of John Jacob Astor.

Moving to another seat, Selena surrendered herself to Myrna for a manicure and pedicure thinking, the woman has a tender brush, but her prattle's distracting due to dentures so ill-fitted they swash and clack. Watching her at work, I recalled that, next to my legs, all three husbands glorified hands and feet as my best features.

I permitted my mind latitude to muse on the days ahead. Offstage encounters with Rolf continue to be awkward; he's become so subdued I miss our earlier banter. At least since the fiasco he no longer flaunts himself in front of Bunny. I wonder, did cobra von Braun or her bogus fiancé notice the incident? Surely not, or they'd have pounced on the morsel like ravenous she-wolves.

Well, such events are insignificant compared to arrangements I must make for the closing night gala. For days I pondered. What might I do to make my party memorably unique? When at last it came to me I rushed to the *Farmer's Almanac*, looked up September 4th, and there it was! The promise there'd be a full moon, which stirred my imagination to romantic notions like—like disguise. Yes! I shall make the party a *bal masque*. Yes, I can see it. I shall order a platform assembled in the water hazard next to the eighteenth green, where an orchestra will perform. I can hear the music, hear the fountain splashing, see the costumed revelers swirling about on a spring-loaded dance floor atop the fairway. Oh! Oh, how Martin would have adored this!

Not so fast, imaginative minx. Be prepared when you propose the concept, the small-minded Greens Committee will shrill complaint, grousing about damage to the grass. What to do? Easy as pie, one-two-three, I'll mollify them with a generous contribution to—what? How about the Employees' Christmas Fund?

If only the Membership Committee could be bought so easily, but alas, the time has passed.

Hugh Tisdale had been laying low since causing the calamitous outage, deciding it prudent to concentrate on his acting career, his role as Gangster Two in *Kiss Me Kate*. The musical was a dream come true because the chorus was composed of the prettiest girls in Loma Bella.

The problem was, in order to impress them, he should take

them to restaurants before performance or bistros after, and this year's trust allowance had been emptied by his fling with the checker at Safeway.

Nothing else to do, he thought. Selena's gotta advance me funds from next year's money.

He broached the subject in her living room. "No dice," she said.

"But look at the favor I've been doing you, sister mine. You think I enjoy this acting silliness? Like yourself, I was raised to believe the stage is for prostitutes and ne'er-do-wells, and here I am, toadying to your Bohemian friends, the incredibly egotistical, untalented rooster Burbage, and the overrated Cornish game hen, Mary Tallmadge."

"You hush!"

"You think either of them would've been invited to dinner by Mumsy and Da-da? Do you, seriously? Yet look at you, treating them as if they're Ari and Jackie Onassis."

He saw he'd scored, because Selena went to the desk and opened her checkbook. "In exchange for remembering your manners, I shall advance you a small portion of next year's sum. But you are not to sully the Tisdale name further with temper tantrums and promiscuity. Do I make myself clear?"

"Perfectly," Hugh said, watching. Waiting for her to tear out the check, he thought, she looks damned good for an old broad. I wonder if she's getting any.

I also wonder which fox is most likely to examine my etchings. I'd better be cautious here. A few of them are underage and could be living at home with hulking, hostile fathers. Nobody enjoys a quickie more than me, but not at cost of my life.

She tore out the check and handed it over. Satisfied with the amount, he pocketed it, saying, "Thanks a bunch, sis." But he couldn't resist a departing jab. "By the way, once the show's history, who's gonna be feeding the free-loading face of Rolf Victor?"

Selena rose and accosted him. "Mr. Victor has worked for every dollar he has ever earned, unlike you. Don't you dare denigrate him. Just take your bribe and leave."

Hugh frowned. "Does this mean I'm not invited to your *bal masque*?"

"Only if you're clever enough to wear a disguise impossible to penetrate. Ever since your costly scene there are men in Elsinore who'd welcome an opportunity to do you physical harm." He grinned indifference. "Your application for club membership is now, of course, out of the question."

He shrugged. "I wouldn't be caught dead rubbing elbows with your Alzheimer patients. La Paloma is the club for me."

"I agree. Your marginal class should blend in well with gasoline attendants. Now kindly disappear as inconspicuously as possible."

Hugh fired a breezy salute. "See ya at work. See ya at the *bal*."

After professional scrutiny Tisdale settled on a dyed blonde as pick of the chorine litter. Her name was Maisie, and she came with compact curves, collagen lips and a smoky voice. She was also something of a wacko. During his reconnaissance Hugh asked, "Where you from?"

And she answered, "Uterus." Stumped, his look begged clarification. "Kidding. It's Utica. I'm from Utica, New York."

Of course even Loma Bella halfwits know the university's a place parents send problem children, but three thousand miles? "Why'd your folks send you so far away?" he asked.

She twined fingers together and placed them between her knees to perform an elaborate shrug. "Beats me." Her laugh was a high-pitched hiccough.

"Maybe you'll have dinner with me some night. You know, before the show?"

Maisie narrowed her eyes. "Hold the phone, mister. You married?" After he shook his head she said, "I dunno. You're kinda old."

For once it was unnecessary for Hugh to pretend hurt. He said, "Forget it, then. I was only trying to be friendly."

She touched his arm in apology, "Aw, I didn't mean—I mean, I'm not mean. Sure, why not? We could grab a bite some night."

Hugh had gone weeks without seminal relief. "Does tomorrow work for you?"

Again the elaborate shrug. "I suppose. What kinda food you have in mind?"

"Up to you."

"I'm into exotic."

Tisdale waggled his eyebrows like Groucho. "The more exotic the better, I always say."

"Then we'll go to my hangout, the Tunisian Palace."

Next evening he stood outside the restaurant awaiting her arrival. Aromas that wafted to his nostrils made him skeptical. As ever dressed for golf, he was unsettled by her appearance in a silk dress. Pointing, he began, "I didn't realize—"

She waved off the apology. "It doesn't matter. Only the food matters."

Opening the door, she preceded him inside. The contrast, leaving sunlight's glare, required an acclimating pause. Soon he discerned in the dark six tables, all empty, each with one burning candle. An Arab emerged from the gloom, bowing to the young woman before kissing her hand. "Miss Maisie," he said.

"Howdy, Akbar."

The waiter held out a chair for her and set down two menus. "Something to drink first?"

"They don't have a liquor license," she warned. "You want wine? It should be a sweet wine to complement the couscous."

"I'm entirely in your pretty hands," said Hugh. He was already regretting the adventure; the joint stank of musty mysteries. "What's that I smell?"

"Spices, mostly. Akbar, we'll have a bottle of Moroccan Mist."

While the raghead was fetching it, Hugh began doing familiar spadework for a successful tryst. "Maisie, you're absolutely the best dancer in the show."

"No, I'm not. Bunny is."

"Well, Bunny has—energy, I guess you'd call it—among other things. Too bad she married such a jerk."

She stiffened, offended. "Look, fella, it's not nice to dis people behind their backs."

Hugh retreated. "You're entirely right, miss. I'm ashamed of myself. Let's get back to talking about you and *your* talent."

She flounced modestly. "Well, it's nice you noticed. Velvet's a super teacher."

He was patting her down with his eyes. "Tell me, how do you keep yourself in such—" using both hands to sculpt curvature from air "—in such incredible shape?"

"Besides dancing, you mean?" He nodded. She frowned, thinking. "Well, now that you mention it, I do exercise quite a bit. I do a lot of fucking."

Tisdale was wiping away sweat with his napkin while the waiter decanted the wine. "Is it me," he asked, "or is it close in here?"

"You like chicken?…Good. Akbar, we'll both have the chicken couscous." She smiled at Hugh. "I warned you, I'm into exotic." She raised her glass. "Allah be praised."

He clinked hers. "Bottoms up." He should have sipped but foolishly swallowed. As it went down he thought, so *this* is what horse piss tastes like. Resisting the temptation to spew it out, he set his mouth in imitation of pleasure.

"You like it?"

After a final gulp he croaked, "It's—well, like you say—it's sure sweet."

"It's to cool the flavor of the coucous."

A politic inquiry was in order. "Just what—what is couscous exactly?"

Her eyes narrowed to frame an accurate reply. "It's a kind of—north African pasta, made from bran, wheat flour, and—well, other delicious things."

"I like pasta," said Hugh guardedly.

"Then you'll love this. Ah—thanks, Akbar." As the waiter set down the two dishes she asked, "Is there plenty of harissa?"

"As always, Miss Maisie, the chef has seasoned it to your taste."

She cut a piece of the chicken and submerged it in a red sauce. Tasting, she groaned pleasure. "Perfect."

Hugh mimicked her, first slicing a mouthful of chicken, then dipping it in the lava-looking sauce. He'd ingested it before the taste kicked in, erupting in his stomach with volcanic fire, evoking a muted scream. *"Ahhhhhh!"*

His eyes were pouring as he lunged for a glass of water, drinking it down to the last ice cube, then snatching Maisie's to do the same. He came up gasping, calling, "Water! More water!"

Akbar rushed to set down a pitcher Hugh gripped in both hands. The waiter and Maisie watched contemptuously as his head disappeared amidst gulping sounds.

When at last it emerged from the empty pitcher, wheezing and gagging, his tryst chided, "It was only spices; just a combination of chilies."

"Jesus. My throat's hamburger, there's still a bonfire in my gut."

"Oh please," said Maisie, tsking. "You're not much of a man, are you?"

"I'm—well, I sure am."

"None of my boyfriends has ever complained. They say harissa helps them get up for the job, if you know what I mean. It sure makes 'em hot, and when they get hot, so do I."

"Excuse it," Hugh garbled, setting two twenties on the table. "Need go home—have show to do."

Maisie performed her elaborate shrug. "See ya, sissy."

In an apartment prepared for consummation of a seduction—lights dimmed, CDs programmed in ascendingly erotic order, Tisdale felt a sudden rush of diarrhea.

Christ, he thought as the couscous departed, no wonder Arabs are so effing cruel. Can you imagine having to eat that shit every day?"

But the man's relief was short-lived. On arrival at the Romero he was seized by a second rush that propelled him like a projectile, from the street, into the lobby, into the nearest restroom, into a stall to lock himself in.

Backstage, Buster Rooney was giving his actors countdown to curtain when he noticed he was missing Gangster Two. He hurried to Mary. "What are we going to do?" the boy asked. "No point checking the Green Room; Hugh never goes in the place. Like Rolf, he never drinks before a performance. We don't have understudies—"

Mary bit her lip. "Quick," she said. "Bring me Baxter."

At his appearance, dressed in pinstripe suit, she asked, "Do you happen to know Hugh's lines?"

It was a perplexing question. "I've listened to them every night. I dunno—well, I suppose—why?"

"Because tonight there won't be two Gangsters. Just you."

It was no optical illusion that her large ex-husband diminished in size.

Then she sent Buster running to find Reggie. While waiting she went to Rolf's dressing room, then Selena's, to warn both of the plan.

Finally, when the director showed up she delivered the dire news. "We're missing Hugh. Do you want to cancel?"

Reggie paled. "We can't do that. We have a full house; the show must go on."

"Then we've got to gamble. We're asking Baxter to be credible speaking two roles." Reggie winced. "Unless, of course, you have an alternative."

He shook his head, then smashed a fist into the palm of his left hand, crying, "Damn! Damn the man! Where on earth do you suppose he can be?"

Tisdale was feeling stronger. He'd flushed away his anguish and was zipping his trousers when he heard female voices in the lobby.

"We should hurry, Esther," one said. "The curtain's due to go up any minute."

"Just a sec. I need to fix my face," the other replied.

Hugh's heart skipped. Idiot! You're in the wrong john! When he heard the outside door open he raised his feet off the floor to conceal male footwear.

"Agnes is saving our seats," said the first voice. "Unless— Agnes, is that you in there?"

No reply.

"Well, I guess not," the first voice said, then laughed. "Whoever the lady is, she's in some distress."

The second woman joined the laughter, saying, "Let's go."

After Hugh heard the door close he eased his feet back on the tile. There was the sound of distant piano, meaning the show had started. What should he do? He visualized his itinerary: From the lobby he needed to go outside, rush all the way around the building to the backstage entrance, then change into wardrobe before his first scene. Baxter must be sweating bullets, he thought.

He let himself out of the cubicle, hurried to the door, opened it a crack to see the coast was clear, then nonchalantly strolled into the lobby.

Reggie was standing at the rear of the orchestra. Seizing the fugitive, he whispered hoarsely, "Hurry, you bloody fool! The show's begun. Run!"

So Hugh ran.

17

THE UNSTABLE framework of the alliance between dowagers Cabot and von Braun came clattering down again thanks to double agent Consuela Gomez.

Again it was the indiscretion of Isobel's fiancé at fault. From Kip's wastebasket the dogged cleaning lady recovered a sheet of paper torn in sixteen pieces. She put them in the pocket of her smock and later, in Little Tijuana, used Scotch tape to join them together like a picture puzzle.

The message, scribbled in ballpoint pen, was a frantic jumble. It read:

Robin Hoodlum,

We had an agreement, bitch! You keep your hands off my hunks, I won't bother yours. Well, when Clyde told me to piss off, that he was leaving me for you, I cried for two days. Just you wait, pussycat. All's fair, and my time will come. I only hope you drown in your own tears, as I almost did.

I hate you,
Wesley

Consuela recognized the name as *Señora* Cabot's hairdresser, so took the evidence to Versailles.

Even as Selena was gloating over ammunition so damaging to Izzy's betrothal pretense, she cocked an eye at the cleaning woman. Have all the skeletons been removed from my closets, I wonder? Best check it out. This lady never studied ethics.

I should be ashamed. A woman of consequence should be able to rise above that snub by Wee Willow, yet it continues to fester. It rankles as the cobra's sole victory, and any victory is unconscionable.

Glancing again at the mutilated letter, she thought, a ball has just been served to my court and is hanging there, ripe for an overhead smash.

Should I?

Does the sun ever shine in Loma Bella?

She lifted the receiver of her Number Memory phone, pressed "Dial," then "2," to hear the voice of confidante Lady Louise. "Dear," Selena began, "can you remember how many years it's been now since darling Isobel announced her engagement to little Kip?"

There was a pause at the other end before Louise replied, "I'm not sure that…Well, she's never actually announced it, has she? But I believe it's been an unofficial understanding ever since Frederick died, which was—"

"Over four years ago." Selena let this sink in before continuing, "Do you happen to recall the occasion when she sent a private detective to Vancouver, hoping to prove Lord Peter's title was bogus? Does that kindle a tiny spark of animosity?"

"Oh!" A sound resembling a blow to the solar plexus. "That hideous woman, that awful, unprincipled witch! I shall never forget nor forgive!"

"Nor do I blame you, love," Selena said. "But you know— Well, she and I are so much a team, as it were, promoting this production of *Kate,* and the performances leave me little opportunity to organize parties. But don't you think someone, sometime, should let Isobel and Kippy know how ecstatic we are they've chosen to plight their troth?"

Lady Louise was on the same page. "But what a splendid idea! Lord Peter and I would love nothing better than to arrange a party here at Vancouver Sunset, a wedding shower for—tupperware, perhaps? Send invitations to all our friends, announcing—"

"A celebration of the impending marriage of Mr. and Mrs. Robin Perkins. No date necessary, darling. No need to be specific."

"Ooh. Selena dear, you *are* wicked."

"One other thing, sweet. When you draw up the invitation list, be sure it includes the name of Wesley Ames?"

After replacing the receiver she paused. She had one more call to make.

Rolf was flattered. At long last his costar held out a social hand, inviting him for an after-theater bite in her home.

Let's go first cabin, Rolfie, he thought as he selected clean denims and a blue button-down shirt. Let's show the lady you have class, he thought as he entered a liquor store. Presenting himself at her front door, he flashed the label of a pricey Cabernet Sauvignon. "For you."

She accepted it, saying, "You shouldn't spend money on me."

He thought, I'll spend whatever it takes, lady, to get in your good graces. A table was set for two in the dining area, candles already aglow. At the wet bar she poured me a double Dewar's, herself champagne from an opened bottle in an ice bucket, and raised it to clink glasses. "*Merde,*" she said.

"*Salud, dinero y mujer.*"

After a smile and a sip, she gestured with a toss of her head. "Care for a tour?"

I followed her expensive gown, again aware such an item would cost me three months' rent. In the hallway I passed paintings, by important artists I supposed, because I recognized a nude by Georgia O'Keeffe. She opened a door, announcing, "My den."

When I stepped inside I heard crackling and saw a welcoming fire. Books lined the walls behind a couch and a comfortable armchair. On a coffee table three framed photographs were on display; I picked up one, an unposed shot of a young Selena in the company of a much older man.

"That's Carter, my first husband." When I looked up she said, "Yes, he was much older, but I loved him; enough, anyway, to give up a theatrical career."

I nodded and picked up a second photo, this of a laughing Selena together with a foreign-looking guy. He stood behind her with his arms locked just under her breasts, grinning lasciviously.

"My second husband. He was an artist."

"Handsome."

As I picked up the third, a formal pose of Selena with a distinguished-looking contemporary, she was already explaining. "And this is Martin. After he died, I gave up all thought of marriage. I'm better off living alone."

She exited the room for the hall and again I followed. She indicated a closed door. "My bedroom. Out of bounds."

But she opened a door across the hall and led the way into an enormous room with two crystal chandeliers, a large dressing table, a chiffonier, walk-in closets, and a bed the size of Rhode Island. "My guest room," she said.

"Wow."

"Actually, it's been unoccupied since 1999, when Count Carlo Vespighi and his wife Contessa Sophia were my houseguests during Fiesta."

I teased, "Your pal Isobel has a nice guest room, but nothing to match this."

"My pal?" She grimaced. "Come. Let's see if Jewel has dinner ready."

You bet she did. Jewel was a coffee-colored gourmet chef. Bowls of *vichysoisse* were accompanied by a dry white wine and and what began as superficial conversation.

"Will you miss doing the show?" I asked.

There was nothing superficial about her reply. "I can't tell you how much," she gushed. "How many people can claim they saw their fondest wish come true, that they were able to fulfill their wildest fantasy? It was heaven. Now I have no notion of what to do with myself; I've created a hole in my life." She exhaled. "Your turn."

"For what?"

"I've shared all my innermost secrets, including my romantic past. What's yours? You currently dating?"

"No." I didn't like where this was going.

"Ever been married?"

"Yeah, once. Jewel, that was scrumptious."

During the *escalopes de veau* with fried potatoes, accompanied by my Cabernet, Selena resumed the interrogation. "Where is it you live in Los Angeles?"

"Oh, near Beverly Hills."

"Beverly Hills has some wonderful restaurants. As a bachelor you must dine out frequently."

"Oh, sure."

"I adore Trader Vic's, don't you?"

"Definitely." I'd never been there. "Jewel, will you marry me?"

I discouraged further chat by wolfing a *salade nicoise*; for dessert I gorged *crepes suzettes*.

Sated, I sat back. "Four stars, my lovely hostess. You've got yourself a Jewel."

Selena smiled. "She spoils me so."

I picked up my wine glass and, sipping, caught her observing me. Maybe it was the candlelight, maybe that elegant dress ("It's a Givenchy"), but at that moment my costar looked more appetizing to me than any *crepes suzettes*.

Her house reeked of money—the furnishings, the paintings, her clothes and jewelry, even her perfume. I had an image of myself a week hence, back in El Segundo, pizza cartons on the floor, wearing tee shirt and skivvies, sitting in front of my TV guzzling a Bud Light. There had to be a better life, and here it was.

Meeting Selena's gaze, wondering if she thought less of me for wearing a toupée, I submitted a tentative smile.

It was answered by a seductive sip of champagne.

18

I'VE HAD IT with the bully, Yolanda thought. Just because Her Royal Highness, Morgan Ball, is in charge of the crew doesn't mean she's entitled to every privilege. I mean, what gives her the right to put dibs on the prettiest girl in the chorus? Here I was, making nice progress with Lucy; she let me hold her hand as she poured her heart out about abuse suffered from insensitive brutes. She was so touched by my sympathy I had her complete trust. In fact, I was on the verge of setting up a dinner date when you-know-who saw us holding hands and connived an excuse to put me to work.

I'd drop it, just let it go, except this isn't the first time the twat has sabotaged me. The first time in this show, yes, but I think of the other times, at the YWCA, muscling me aside to claim the shower next to a yum-yum I had my eye on.

Well, this time she's gone too far and I'm gonna make her pay. The mighty muck-a-muck lords it over everybody because the director smothers her with compliments, telling her how indispensable she is, how completely reliable, "the show wouldn't be the success it is without you," and all that crap. Because she stands over six-two and phony Burbage only comes up to her hooters, he's more cowed than grateful.

So I've decided to level the playing field. I can't get even by fouling up the scene changes because it'd be obvious. No, something else has to go wrong, something that happens when I'm not around, maybe even when *she's* not around. And when the idea finally came to me, I couldn't help it; I had to giggle.

The perfect booby trap's right there in plain sight of God and everybody, a permanent part of the backstage set—the pay telephone outside the doorman's office. It's used only three times in the show, but if it malfunctioned it'd cause holy hell. I asked myself, what if I unscrewed the bolts—just loosened them, so that at some point, during some performance, unknown to the actor or even to me, when the receiver's picked up the whole damn thing comes out of the wall?

It'd be a crashing surprise, bound to give Ball a case of redass. That spotless reputation of hers would get smeared, for sure.

So after a Saturday performance, when everybody was in a rush to claim a stool over at the Green Room, I lagged behind. After the stage door slammed, I took a wrench out of my tool belt and went to work, loosening each of the four bolts half a crank. Then I split for the bar.

When more than a week passed with no result, it made me think I'd screwed up. Until the night I heard a loud gasp from the audience. Bunny was doing her 'I'm Always True To You In My Fashion' number, where she picks up the phone receiver to sing into it, and bingo—the contraption came off the wall. Luckily she skipped away or it could've broken a foot, but being a trouper, she smiled and pretended it was a gag, an intended part of the show, never missing a note.

Well, har-de-har, another kind of note is what mighty Morgan got from furious Reg. He wouldn't allow her to tower over him; he had her sit down before he got in her face, his Brit diction washing her in a shower of rage. The sight of the moose shrinking in her seat made me put a hand over my mouth to keep from laughing out loud.

Tit for tat, Ball baby, if you know what I mean.

Kiss Me Kate had but two nights remaining in the run and Ned Jarvis had yet to see it. His excuse—"Me and the missus watch only TV"—was a lie. If he had to look at Mooney dancing and listen to the applause, he'd throw up. Crap like that wasn't in the line of duty.

Showing up in Elsinore's club dining room *was* in the line of duty. The place was a mess of boxes and tissue paper. He stood to one side, watching staff as they hung posters on the wall, photos of old-time movie stars.

I've got to hand it to Otto, he thought. Always comes up with nifty ideas to coddle the membership.

Speak of the devil—here he comes, in a suit I never saw before, but then I can't remember seeing him wearing the same suit twice. I said, "I see that tomorow night we'll be going to the movies."

Otto sounded smug. "That's the general idea."

"There'll be a mob of people; the joint'll be jumping. You have any security concerns?"

The manager reached to unpack rolls of confetti. "The members have avoided attacking one other so far—physically, that is."

The statement nudged a thought to my mouth. "While we're on the subject, maybe you can tell me. When do you suppose the stupid feud between the two hellcats is gonna end?"

Otto reacted as if the answer were obvious and said something prophetic. "Only after one has destroyed the other."

✿   ✿   ✿

The seamstresses at Free Your Fantasy were never busier than in the days preceding Selena Cabot's closing party. The demand for costumes was so overwhelming, the requests so varied, calls were made to wardrobe departments at Paramount, Warner Brothers, and Universal, all of whom charged outrageous fees for the rentals.

Rolf Victor assumed he was exempt, until he received an unexpected backstage visitation. "What in hell are you doing here?" he asked Anastasia Popkin.

She said, "Thought I'd drop by for the closing festivities; I'm in charge of your wardrobe."

Rolf sensed where this was going. "Oh no, you're not. I am not renting an idiot costume. Forget it."

The ferret-faced agent exhaled frustration. "I've already paid for Thomas Jefferson. And for myself I've already paid for Mata Hari. Believe me, you will look terrific as Thomas Jefferson, even better than you did as Petruchio."

"No way, lady."

"I thought you liked your costar."

"I do. We get along like gangbusters."

"Well, look at it this way—it'll give Mrs. Cabot untold pleasure."

Oh. That was different. Now that Rolf had reached the end of their association, he was of a mind to give Mrs. Cabot pleasure of any description. He suspected she'd forgiven his toupée, that indeed she might now be of a mind to welcome courteous advances. In fact, he believed if ever he got a toe in the door of Mrs. Cabot's bedroom, it would crumble like the Berlin Wall.

Anastasia was saying, "It's no big deal. Tomorrow you can go home; you'll never have to see this town again."

"Ah, but maybe I will, my little Popkin." Addressing her confusion, he added, "Now where exactly am I to be fitted for the Jeffersonian codpiece?"

AROUND THE BLOCK
Caitlin Wills

The Elsinore Country Club is abuzz in anticipation of the *bal masque* that will take place after the closing performance of *Kiss Me Kate.*

Selena Cabot, so vibrant in the title role, is hostess for this event, and promises we shall have occasion to meet and congratulate her costar, **Rolf Victor**, as well as the new sensation, **Bunny Auchincloss**, together with her husband, **Arthur**.

We should all be grateful to **Isobel von Braun** for her generous financial support of this smash hit. It has given **Reggie Burbage** opportunity for enthusiastic amateurs to demonstrate they can hold their own with professionals.

Case in point: the singing and dancing of Loma Bella's own **Robin Perkins**!

And kudos to UCLB students who participated prominently in the musical. Take a bow, **Perry Nelson**, **Marci Dusek**, **Tad Wismer** and **Chauncey Slater**!

You've made the show a block party!

Otto outdid himself redecorating the clubhouse for *Kiss Me Kate*'s closing night gala. Using silent films as his motif, he ordered portrait posters hung on the dining room walls, tributes to stars of yesteryear like Chaplin, Keaton, Douglas Fairbanks, Theda Bara, Valentino, and Lillian Gish. He personally footed the bill at Wesley's Salon to have the hair of female staff cut and styled in keeping with their dress as flappers, and he obtained uniforms for the men to impersonate Keystone Kops.

Outside on the terrace he stationed a sextet to play animated Charleston rhythms. Following dinner, the group would perform on a bandstand erected in the water hazard by the eighteenth green. Of course, musicians need occasional breaks, so Otto arranged that Roaring Twenties recordings be piped in for nonstop melodic jubilation.

Two by two the members entered the clubhouse in high-pitched excitement, exclaiming over originality of transparent disguises. No mask could conceal familiar voices and mannerisms, and some costumes required no speculation at all. Who else but Baxter Clarke would come as Arnold Schwarzenegger, in Terminator garb? Who else but Trevor Faye would come as W.C. Fields, with a pocket device that lit up his putty nose? Who else but Lord Peter Glenn would come as Ben Hogan, in signature cap and plus fours?

Reggie Burbage was more difficult to identify because few guests were familiar with the plays of Oscar Wilde. He was masquerading as Algernon from *The Importance of Being Earnest*, while Daisy was bedecked as Lady Bracknell.

Guests gravitated automatically to Table One to greet their hostess, but Selena wasn't there.

Instead they saw Table One presided over by Orphan Annie, Isobel von Braun in a curly orange wig with freckles painted on her cheeks. Ashley Faye was Tinkerbell, in tutu and tiara, bestowing blessings with a fairy wand, while Baxter Clarke's wife, Libby, though outsized for a jockey, had exchanged piano for racing silks, carrying a riding crop that inspired speculation about bedtime at Bowflex.

But it was Table One's host who caused the room's greatest stir. "How can you permit this?" Isobel was asked, indicating her fiancé's costume.

"How can I not?" was the arch reply. "It gives the tyke such innocent pleasure."

The reference was to Kip Perkins masquerading as Monica Lewinski, in a shoulder-length wig and pink dress with a large stain, his mouth drawn in cherry lip gloss to resemble that of the notorious intern.

Masked eyes that scanned the room, ears alert for the voice of Selena Cabot, were confounded. "Where on earth do you suppose our hostess is hiding herself?" Mary Tallmadge asked her husband.

Naturally there was no reply. Judge Horace was masquerading as Ludwig von Beethoven so he could dispense with the bother of hearing aids; they were in a drawer at home.

Who could have guessed the hostess had skipped dinner altogether? Selena was immersing herself in the rewards of scrupulous planning, watching dancers twist, shake, and twirl on the spring-loaded floor, under a sky full of stars, the full moon augmented by Klieg lights.

No one heeded Mother Teresa as she strolled past refreshment tables. Caitlin Wills, attired in mufti, a paisley cocktail dress with omnipresent Press badge, wouldn't have noticed in any event, scribbling in her pad, avid to unmask revelers.

"Who's that?" she asked a Royal Canadian Mounted Policeman, pointing to a cocked-hat Napoleon.

"Unless I'm mistaken," the Mountie said, "it's Lady Louise Glenn."

"Ah!" More scribbling. "I should have guessed, dancing with Ben Hogan."

Anastasia Popkin, masquerading as Mata Hari, glanced to

verify Thomas Jefferson hadn't defected. No, she saw he remained amidst the rejoicing, Carol Channing in his arms.

Still undetected was the individual masquerading as Charlie Chan. Under the straw hat, beneath the drooping Fu Manchu mustache, behind the dental insert that projected buck teeth, lurked Hugh Tisdale. When people smiled he bobbed his head, took a hissing inspiration of breath and said, "Ah so. Velly good. Ah so."

Of course, the bounder was looking for Bunny Auchincloss, hoping to cop a feel in the claustrophobic crush. But Bunny had prepared herself for mischief. She was the nine-month-pregnant Serb peasant under the dirty kerchief with a wart on her nose.

Pointing at her, Caitlin asked the Mountie, "Can you guess who that is?"

He shrugged. "Beats me. But the other one, the guy wearing a cardboard ATM machine? That'd be Arthur Auchincloss."

Meantime, as proof he was an agreeable star, Rolf Victor accepted invitations to dance from any woman who asked, including this lady in the blonde wig with the wide mouth. Her hand was somewhat rough to the touch, but he reminded himself there were, after all, people who worked for a living.

Pointing at him, Caitlin asked "Who's Thomas Jefferson?"

"Rolf Victor, of course. And the lady—well, I happen to know for a fact it's a hairdresser named Wesley Ames."

Caitlin so whooped with laughter she dropped her pad. After recovering breath she gasped, "Please… Please tell me… I've got to know who you are."

The Mountie lowered his mask to reveal spectacles. "Ms. Wills," he said, "my name is Seymour Katz. You wouldn't know me, but for months I have worshipped you from afar. I've never dared approach because, candidly, many consider me a nebbish and I was afraid you'd find me a bore." He stooped and recovered her pad.

"Thank you. Now tell me, Mr. Katz—"

"It's Doctor Katz. I'm a doctor."

"Thank you. Your opinion of me is highly flattering, but please indulge me. I'm dying to learn how you know Carol Channing is a man."

Katz paused, balanced on a high wire between discretion and desire. Unbalanced by desire, he confided softly, "I am a cosmetic surgeon, Ms. Wills. I beg you, don't betray a confidence, but six months ago I peformed a tush tuck on Mr. Ames."

Awed, Caitlin shook her head. "You must know more secrets than anyone in Elsinore."

"I do, in fact. But please, as much as I want to impress you, don't inquire further. My office is a confessional."

"Understood." She tapped her pen on the pad. "But I have a job to do and would appreciate further assistance. The identity, please, of the tall person dressed as an Indian?"

After a look he said, "Ah. That would be the sculptress Morgan Ball. She was raised in the Dakotas, you see, and is masquerading as a Sioux maiden."

During scribbling: "But why the bandage wrapped over the buckskin on her leg?"

"It's a symbolic protest, I believe. Wounded Knee."

"Oh." Using her pen she pointed at Charlie Chan. "And that would be—?"

Seymour frowned. "I can't recall I ever worked on him, if it is a him."

Their curiosity was answered by an adjoining voice. "It is Hugh Tisdale, the scourge of Elsinore, and I promise you he's up to no damned good."

Both turned to see Albert Einstein, in a frightwig of white hair, with a bushy white mustache. Caitlin asked, "And you, sir, are—?"

Bulldog Jarvis lacked time to respond, burning rubber from

the soles of his Adidas to lay hands on the oriental standing at the water hazard's edge. His swift advance coincided with Charlie Chan's penetration of Bunny's disguise.

"Ah so," he hissed. "Velly good. Phony belly. Velly solly, no fool Cholly Chan."

Embracing her from behind, fondling the pillow padding, his hands were working their way north to test the ripeness of the melons when checked by Albert Einstein.

Grabbing cloth at the nape of Tisdale's neck, along with a handful of trouser seat, Bulldog whirled the scum for a frog-march to captivity. Startled, Chan flailed his arms, one striking Ludwig von Beethoven, the benign Horace Tallmadge. Knocked akilter by the blow, the Judge reached out to right himself, grabbing the arm of a toppling Tisdale, who took Bulldog along for the ride. All three disappeared in a thunderous cannonball.

Standing soaked at the hazard's edge, Caitlin and Seymour studied floating wigs and false facial hair, she scribbling identities of thrashing victims, the Mountie offering rescue with an ineffectual hand.

As the sopping unfortunates crawled to terra firma, the band continued playing "Are You Havin' Any Fun?"

Prepared as always for the unexpected, Otto Steiner materialized, bearing blankets from the clubhouse. He used one to cover shivering Beethoven, and was offering another to Einstein when waved off. Chan had wrenched loose from his grip on the collar and was running for his life. Bulldog whipped out his cell phone to call for backup, only to learn its batteries were waterlogged.

The security chief was gnashing his teeth in frustration. There was nothing he could do; the swine seemed certain of escape. Then agnostic Jarvis became a religious convert, witness to divine intervention.

From under a stand of trees a golf cart emerged, driven by Mata Hari. Anastasia Popkin was so enraged by Chan's harassment of innocent Bunny Auchincloss, she was determined to give the creep a taste of his own medicine. Hugh Tisdale was in the sights of her hood ornament when she put the pedal to the metal; it made contact with his pumping buttocks and planted him like a sack of compost. Anastasia had hit but did not run, in the process of making a U turn for another sortie when Bulldog arrived and held up his arms as plea she stop.

All the fight had gone out of the groaning bastard. Gripping him again by the collar, Jarvis pushed him to the back seat of a waiting security car. "Take this rat to the gatehouse," he ordered the driver. "Cuff him and have him locked up for disturbing the peace."

19

SELENA HAD HEARD splashing, but mercifully was spared viewing the calamity. It was important to her the *bal* should come off without incident because, thanks to Hugh's earlier transgressions, she sensed she was losing the high ground to awful Isobel.

So she supposed the splashing emanated from the gay fountain, and allowed herself to be whirled by a succession of masked partners.

All were unfamiliar to her—until Thomas Jefferson cut in. "Will you hear my confession, Sister Cabot?" It was an unmistakable voice, one she'd heard every night for the past two months.

Selena pealed delightedly. "Naughty man! You're the first to have guessed who I am."

"No mask can conceal those hazel eyes."

Too regal to be won so easily, she chose a nautical metaphor. "I see. Now that Mrs. Auchincloss has rejected you, it's any old port in a storm."

He ignored the rebuke. "Which of my wigs do you prefer? This or the other?"

The self-deprecation drained the dregs of her resistance. "I'm sorry you were embarrassed. The incident meant nothing to me."

"Truly?"

"Why should it? You're a handsome man regardless."

He stopped dancing. "If you can find it in your heart to forgive a wretched imbecile, I'd like to start all over again. May I? Might I introduce myself? My name is Rolf."

She accepted his extended hand. "An unusual name, sir. Isn't it something people do to express what they call 'tough love'?"

Again he ignored her. "And your name is—?"

"Selena."

"Fitting. A beautiful name for a beautiful woman." She lowered her eyes in maidenly modesty. "Selena, may I be so bold as to buy you a glass of your own champagne?"

The hostess left her party early, on the arm of Thomas Jefferson. Masks had been discarded, the band was playing slower, more romantic music, when the exit was observed by columnist Caitlin Wills, cheek to cheek with a Royal Canadian Mounted Policeman.

She said, "I have a suspicion Mother Teresa has no notion of brother Charlie Chan's misbehavior."

"Don't spoil her evening," Seymour murmured. "If my eyes don't deceive me, she's soon to be rewarded. It's the fulfillment of every girl's fantasy, a night of love with a celebrity."

Caitlin waved to the backs of the departing couple. "Night-night, Selena. Have fun."

And Seymour, remembering his youthenasia, commented, "For sure, she'll be looking good."

Inside Versailles, door bolted behind them, Rolf turned to Selena and the two fed on each other's lips like famished trout.

Breathing heavily, Rolf said, "Your place or mine?"

She took his hand, led him to her bedroom, and switched on the light to reveal a bed the size of Ghana. Coquettishly she kissed a finger and pressed it to his lips. "I shall join you in a moment, my heart."

In the bathroom she undressed to admire Dr. Katz's mirrored miracle. God bless him, she thought. As ribbon to this gorgeous gift, she reached for an atomizer of Joy and sprayed herself from neck to toe.

The bedroom was dark when she reappeared, yet she sensed her lover's presence waiting on the bed. Uncertain if she was expected to initiate the event, she asked, "You want a bathroom light on?"

His reply was to rise and clasp her. Feeling naked readiness pressed to her skin, she asked coyly, "Does this mean I'm going to get Rolfed?"

"But gently," he said, and kissed her.

The clamor of her bedside telephone wakened Lady Louise Glenn. Her digital clock informed her it was three-fourteen.

"Who the hell—?" Lord Peter growled.

Louise switched on the lamp. "Yes? Hello? Who on earth—?"

There was a piteous sob from the other end. "Sweetest, you must come at once! The most dreadful thing imaginable has occurred. I need your help desperately!"

The line went dead.

Louise clambered out of bed, groping for her robe. "Selena is in some sort of difficulty. I must fly to her!"

Moonlight bathed the fairways as her slippers bustled the distance from Vancouver Sunset to the front door of Versailles. It was ajar when she arrived, Selena waiting in yellow terrycloth, face swollen with tears.

Louise had an awful premonition. "What is it, darling?"

"It's Rolf Victor. Oh Louise, Louise, the man is dead!" Her moan was drowned in a torrent of tears.

"Are you sure? Perhaps—in any event, we must call 911 at once!" As she scurried to the hall telephone, Selena arrested her.

"No! No, we must not, we cannot. Come see for yourself!" She led Louise to her bed. Atop the covers, a towel draped over his privates, lay the star.

"Oh. Oh, dear. Are you certain he's gone?" Louise asked breathlessly. "I mean, how did this hap—? Never mind, I'll check for a pulse." And she did, feeling first a wrist, then the carotid artery of his neck. "Oh dear, Selena. The man is gone. Oh, dear. What shall we do?"

Selena's agitated reply was virtually incoherent. "For a start, we must get him out of here, out of my bedroom, don't you understand? Out, out, out!" She massaged her temples, pondering frantically. "Yes…Tonight I invited him to be my houseguest. Yes, he accepted…was readying himself for bed, don't you see? That's why we must transport him somehow to—yes, to the guest room, where—where I can pretend—pretend to discover him this morning!"

Louise studied the deceased skeptically. "But how? I mean, he's too heavy—"

Selena bent down and grasped one of Rolf's ankles. "Here, here, hurry, hurry, we must drag him as best we can."

"I don't think—" Louise began, then seeing her friend's panic, took the other ankle.

"Right, then," Selena said. "Ready? One, two, *pull!*"

Rolf Victor crashed to the floor.

"And—*pull*!" Selena ordered, a coxswain commanding her oars.

The women dragged him, then paused for breath.

"And—*pull*!"

By fits and starts the star was dragged on his back, the towel to preserve modesty long gone, the women averting their gaze from his flopping appendage.

The acclaimed musical star paused to recover breath. She was moaning as she raised her tear-streaked face to heaven. "Oh my Lord! Please God, I promise! I promise that never, ever again, as long as I live, will I loose this weapon of mass destruction on mankind. I promise, I promise!"

"Oh, be still," snapped Louise. "Just shut up, and *pull*!"

To get him through the doorway to the guest room they needed to turn Rolf on his side and yank him through. Looking about, her mind at full throttle, Selena commanded, "To the bathroom! Yes! He had a—a stroke or something while taking a shower!"

Both ladies were puffing hard when Lady Louise gasped, "Let me see. How did you—why did you—yes. You wakened in the middle of the night, worried you'd left no soap in the guest bathroom, and—"

Selena fleshed out the alibi. "Yes, he'd just stepped out of the shower, don't you see, when—Wait. First we must run the water, get the tiles wet—" The splattering reminded her. "Wait! Now it's his turn." She filled a glass from the sink and splashed the contents all over him, then did it a second time. "Next? Towel! Yes, he needed to dry himself, didn't he, when—" And she draped one over his manliness. She paused, bosom heaving, wondering if she'd neglected anything.

Watching, Lady Louise asked, "Now?"

"Now? Now what?"

"Now do you call 9u? We've got to—to do it sooner than later, dear."

Selena touched the guest room telephone but couldn't bring herself to lift it, paralyzed by terror of tomorrow.

When she mustered courage to press the three numbers, Lady Louise was suddenly galvanized. "Wait, wait, for God's sake wait! You are alone. There is no one else here. I am gone. I have never known a single particular of this frightful event!"

As evidence, she fled the scene.

20

BULLDOG JARVIS was helpless to deny incursion by Cuffs Mooney. Whenever 9u is dialed the emergency becomes a city matter, out of the jurisdiction of Elsinore security.

Privately it came as no surprise at all to Jarvis the star had croaked at Versailles. If Bunny Auchincloss didn't want him, he'd just make a minor change of plan. It was only a matter of time before he wised up to what's common knowledge: In Elsinore, at the end of every widow's driveway, you find a pot of gold.

The fathead got what was coming to him, Bulldog thought. I don't buy the newspaper story he had a heart attack taking a shower; I'd bet my pension he died in the saddle. But I can never prove it, of course, because Cuffs is going to sit on the coroner's report.

Can you give me another reason for Mrs. Cabot's twenty-five thousand dollar donation to the police Big Brother Fund? Everybody in Loma Bella with an IQ above room temperature knows the score, including her scuzz brother after she bailed him out of the slammer.

Her excuse, published in the *Sun*, was that Tisdale had been punished enough and furthermore is irreplaceable in the projected touring company of *Kiss Me Kate*. Sure. And my name is Bill Gates. So I did some digging and found out she's rented him an apartment in Gila Bend, Arizona, the hottest place you'll find, next to hell, and as tradeoff for a bigger trust allowance got him to sign a document promising never, ever to return to Loma Bella, or else model the orange jump suit they issue at Lompoc prison.

Good riddance.

AROUND THE BLOCK

Caitlin Wills

It is with mixed feelings that your editor reports this is her final column.

Mixed, because I shall miss the loyal support of all you readers, as well as your company at Loma Bella social functions.

Mixed, because it is my joy to announce impending nuptials to **Dr. Seymour Katz** in September on the Elsinore clubhouse terrace. My daughter **Daphne**, formally adopted by my new husband, will serve as maid of honor, and **Otto Steiner** has graciously agreed to serve as best man.

Following a honeymoon in Mexico, during which **Seymour** and I plan to track the migration of Monarch butterflies, we shall move into our new home, Nips and Tucks, just off the seventh green on Claudius Corner.

So, good friends, this is not "goodbye" but rather *"au revoir."*

You will find our door is always open.

Addled by her calamity, Selena Cabot completely forgot to cancel invitations to a wedding shower honoring the impending nuptials of Mr. and Mrs. Robin Perkins.

Isobel von Braun was made to suffer the humiliation of doing that herself, telephoning each and every proposed guest with an implausible explanation of this misunderstanding.

However, there was no doubt whose devious mind had concocted the scheme. Isobel decided that retribution needed to be exceptionally cruel. Accordingly, she mailed a check to Chief Mooney sufficient to finance police charities for at least the next decade, in exchange for four pieces of paper—copies of three death certificates and a recent autopsy.

Otto's prophecy had come true.

Conceding she'd relinquished rights to Table One forever, recently deified Selena Cabot seldom dined out anymore. But when she did, if Isobel von Braun happened to capture her eye, four fingers were thrust in the air.

Message received, the *grande dame* of Versailles shuddered.